THE FOLGER LIBRARY
SHAKESPEARE

Designed to make Shakespeare's classic plays available to the general reader, each edition contains a reliable text with modernized spelling and punctuation, scene-by-scene plot summaries, and explanatory notes clarifying obscure and obsolete expressions. An interpretive essay and accounts of Shakespeare's life and theater form an instructive preface to each play.

Louis B. Wright, General Editor, was the Director of the Folger Shakespeare Library from 1948 until his retirement in 1968. He is the author of *Middle-Class Culture in Elizabethan England, Religion and Empire, Shakespeare for Everyman,* and many other books and essays on the history and literature of the Tudor and Stuart periods.

Virginia Lamar, Assistant Editor, served as research assistant to the Director and Executive Secretary of the Folger Shakespeare Library from 1946 until her death in 1968. She is the author of *English Dress in the Age of Shakespeare* and *Travel and Roads in England,* and coeditor of William Strachey's *Historie of Travell into Virginia Britania.*

The Folger Shakespeare Library

GENERAL EDITOR

LOUIS B. WRIGHT

Director, Folger Shakespeare Library, 1948–1968

ASSISTANT EDITOR

VIRGINIA A. LaMAR

Executive Secretary, Folger Shakespeare Library, 1946–1968

The Folger Library General Reader's Shakespeare

MEASURE FOR MEASURE

by

WILLIAM SHAKESPEARE

WSP

WASHINGTON SQUARE PRESS
PUBLISHED BY POCKET BOOKS NEW YORK

A Washington Square Press Publication of
POCKET BOOKS, a division of Simon & Schuster, Inc.
1230 Avenue of the Americas, New York, N.Y. 10020

ISBN: 0-671-49612-3

First Pocket Books printing March, 1965

15 14 13 12 11 10 9 8

Preface

This edition of *Measure for Measure* is designed to make available a readable text of one of Shakespeare's lesser-known plays. In the centuries since Shakespeare, many changes have occurred in the meanings of words, and some clarification of Shakespeare's vocabulary may be helpful. To provide the reader with necessary notes in the most accessible format, we have placed them on the pages facing the text that they explain. We have tried to make these notes as brief and simple as possible. Preliminary to the text we have also included a brief statement of essential information about Shakespeare and his stage. Readers desiring more detailed information should refer to the books suggested in the references, and if still further information is needed, the bibliographies in those books will provide the necessary clues to the literature of the subject.

The early texts of Shakespeare's plays provide only scattered stage directions and no indications of setting, and it is conventional for modern editors to add these to clarify the action. Such additions, and additions to entrances and exits, as well as many indications of act and scene division, are placed in square brackets.

All illustrations are from material in the Folger Library collections.

L. B. W.
V. A. L.

July 7, 1964

Humane versus Legal Justice

Few of Shakespeare's plays have aroused more diverse and contradictory interpretations than *Measure for Measure*. Nineteenth-century critics violently condemned it as a callous and inhuman play, reflecting some deep emotional disturbance and disillusionment in the author. Other critics have seen in it a reflection of the cynicism characteristic, they think, of the Jacobean age. It has been classified as a "dark" or "problem" comedy, bordering more upon tragedy than upon comedy. More recent critics have taken a less unfavorable view of the play; they argue that it shows the author's concern with humane rather than legalistic justice, that it provides an ending emphasizing mercy and reconciliation. Still others point out that it could not reflect the cynicism of the Jacobean age because no such cynicism existed in the first year of James I's reign, when this play was produced, for James's accession brought the hope of peace and a release from the dread and uncertainty that existed in the last few years of Elizabeth's reign.

In considering *Measure for Measure*, it is well to keep in mind that the term "comedy" did not necessarily imply a play with a predominantly comic spirit but merely one with an ending that saw the main characters alive—and preferably about to be

married. Although obviously *Measure for Measure*
is no joyous comedy, it may be doubted whether its
somber tone indicates a personal tragedy or some
vexing problem in Shakespeare's own life. It may
merely represent a mature man's reflections upon the
workings of legal justice in relation to human frailty,
the result of observation and experience that might
come to any individual in any period. Shakespeare,
we should remember, had now reached the age of
forty; and a man of forty in early-seventeenth-cen-
tury England would have seen much that would
stimulate his thinking about the operation of the
law. Clearly Shakespeare was in a thoughtful and
reflective mood when he wrote *Measure for Measure;* but it does not follow that he set himself the
task of adducing answers to all the problems that
he posed, or that he logically planned to give each
of the principal dramatis personae a symmetrical
consistency to illustrate some complexity in human
character, or that he undertook to make his play
into a treatise on moral problems.

Literary critics frequently write as if they thought
Shakespeare fancied himself a professor in whatever
branch of learning his play seems to illustrate, in
the case of *Measure for Measure*, a professor of
ethics and philosophy. Shakespeare, as we shall have
occasion to repeat, was writing for the public stage
as a practical dramatist, albeit an inspired one.
His primary purpose was to produce a play that
would please and interest his audience, and it was
not his intention to turn out a moral tract.

Yet critics of the romantic period, beginning with Samuel Taylor Coleridge, wrote as if they thought Shakespeare had betrayed the moral order in *Measure for Measure*. They could find little good in the play. The behavior of its characters did not fit their conception of the way Christian ladies and gentlemen, even in faraway Vienna, should conduct themselves. Coleridge regarded the play as almost a total offense, because of its cruelty, lust, and baseness. Swinburne was even more vehement and condemned it for its lack of high moral convictions, particularly because in the end the dramatist declines to let poetic justice prevail. The archvillain is forgiven and suffers no worse fate than being forced to marry the girl whose dowry he had earlier found unsatisfactory. Some commentators were horrified that Claudio, under sentence of death and knowing that his life could be saved at the cost of his sister's honor, in a moment of weakness begged her to make the sacrifice. Others were equally disturbed over Isabella's "priggishness" at refusing to rescue her brother by becoming Angelo's mistress. Still others were shocked at the "immorality" of Isabella's finding a substitute in Mariana. To early-nineteenth-century and Victorian critics scarcely a character in the play could live up to the standards required of abstract virtue.

But Shakespeare was not dealing with abstract virtue—or with abstract iniquity. As always in his plays, his characters take on qualities of reality and react as men and women might in situations of

actual life. Claudio reveals himself as no model of
high courage when he breaks down in the face of
death and begs his sister to save him, but his is a
human rather than a story-book reaction, and Shakespeare knew enough about humankind to realize
that Claudio's behavior was not improbable. Shakespeare was also aware of the impact of stern Christian teaching upon a girl of Isabella's type: to Isabella, creeping into Angelo's bed, even to save her
brother, would be a mortal sin involving the destruc-
tion of her own soul. It was not priggishness that
kept her from making the sacrifice but the acceptance of a Christian code that had become a part
of her whole being. She was the stuff that martyrs
are made of, and martyrs were not unknown in
Shakespeare's day. Mariana may not be the sort of
girl who would make a popular heroine in senti-
mental fiction, but Shakespeare reveals her as deeply
in love with Angelo and willing to go to any length
to get him. To provide moral justification for her
willingness to substitute for Isabella in Angelo's
bed, Shakespeare explains that she had been betrothed to him and hence, in effect, was his wife.
Women in Shakespeare's time and later have won
their men in fashions no less devious. Other characters, as they act out their parts on the stage, give
the illusion of reality. The loose-tongued Lucio, getting himself into trouble by maligning the disguised Duke, is reminiscent of Falstaff, while Pompey and Elbow provide the kind of realistic low
comedy demanded by Shakespeare's audiences.

Shakespeare was writing a play to entertain a diverse audience in the public playhouse, and he was using plot material filled with conventional details already familiar in contemporary fiction and drama. For example, the "bed trick" was a motif that had appeared in other plays and in tales translated from Italian into English. Other elements in the play were a part of the folklore of the time. Shakespeare was not inventing morbid scenes and situations because he was despondent and disillusioned with the world. A busy playwright, he picked up popular material and wove it into a play that shows evidence of haste in composition rather than a careful concentration upon every line to produce such a close-knit philosophic tract as some commentators would have us believe Shakespeare sat down to write.

The play changes its tone near the middle, and the second half introduces low comedy scenes with Pompey, Elbow, and Froth and the dramatic irony of Lucio's self-convicting dispraise of the Duke. This shift in tone has produced some discontent among critics who think the low comedy is out-of-place and jarring. But it takes little imagination to conceive of Heminges and Condell—or others of Shakespeare's colleagues in the playhouse—looking over the script and saying, "We have to get some laughs into this thing. Can't you put a flat-footed constable like Dogberry in some of these scenes; and why not get a little of Falstaff into Lucio? If you don't lighten up the last half of the play, it's going to be a failure." So Shakespeare, being a sensible fellow mindful of the box office, put in some humor for the groundlings and satisfied his colleagues. The humor is not so boisterous as that in *Henry IV,* nor is there any of the silvery laughter that ripples through the lighter comedies, but humor there is in *Measure for Measure,* and it is a more effective play because of it.

Although we cannot believe that Shakespeare abdicated his place as practical playwright and took upon himself the role of professor of ethics in *Measure for Measure,* clearly moral and ethical problems engaged his serious interest. The problem that is uppermost in the author's mind, as he portrays moral conditions in Vienna and the Duke's curious methods of righting them, is the conflict between the spirit of the law and the letter of the law. He is profoundly concerned with the impact upon human beings of abstract justice when the rigors of the law are applied by a zealot. This problem was no theoretical proposition for academic discussion but something very real in Shakespeare's as well as every man's experience. Claudio's situation may have reminded the author of the circumstances of his own marriage. Certainly he was not dealing with abstractions in this treatment of human frailties and the laws concerning sexual behavior.

Implicit in the characterization and action of the play is a plea for tolerance and understanding of the nature of human emotions. Whatever may be the stern provisions of the Mosaic code (the imagined code of the dramatist's Vienna) in its efforts to regulate sexual behavior, humane justice requires the application of mercy, the forgiveness vouchsafed by the New Testament, Shakespeare is saying. He is also voicing his contempt for the hypocrisy of the Pharisees and all the hosts of the self-righteous who find it easy to condemn others for sins they themselves secretly practice.

A brilliant essay on the meaning of *Measure for Measure*, delivered in 1937 as a British Academy Lecture by R. W. Chambers under the title, "The Jacobean Shakespeare and *Measure for Measure*," refutes the notion that the play is an expression of disillusionment and cynicism and argues that it is an expression of Shakespeare's recognition of certain tenets of Christian doctrine and Christian charity, as revealed in the New Testament. In *Measure for Measure*, Chambers asserts, Shakespeare reveals that "there are things more important, for oneself and for others, than avoiding death and pain," and he quotes two lines of a Chinese poem that he believes also illustrate the spirit of the play:

It is better to be a crystal and be broken
Than to remain perfect like a tile upon the
    housetop.

Whether one agrees with Chambers that *Measure for Measure* is a play of forgiveness expressing the Christianity of the New Testament, one does not need to go to the other extreme and agree with the nineteenth-century critics who saw in it only evil. It is serious and often solemn, but it portrays human

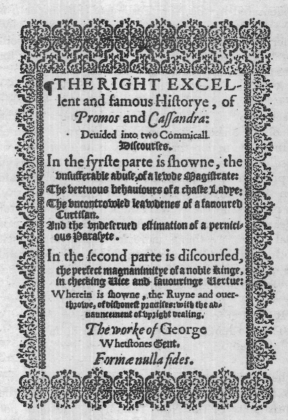

¶THE RIGHT EXCEL-
lent and famous Historye , of
Promos and *Caſſandra*:

Deuided into two Commicall
Diſcourſes.

In the fyrſte parte is ſhowne , the
vnſufferable abuſe, of a lewde Magiſtrate:
The vertuous behauiours of a chaſte Ladye:
The vncontrowled leawdenes of a fauoured
Curtiſan.
And the vndeſerued eſtimation of a pernici-
ous Paraſyte.

In the ſecond parte is diſcourſed,
the perfect magnanimitye of a noble kinge,
in checking Uice and fauouringe Uertue:

Wherein is ſhowne , the Ruyne and ouer-
throwe, of diſhoneſt practiſes: with the ad-
uauncement of vpright dealing.

The worke of George
Whetſtones Gent.

Formæ nulla fides.

Title page of George Whetstone, *Promos and Cassandra* (1578),
one of the prime sources for *Measure for Measure*.

beings as they frequently are, not as moral lecturers might like to have them. In the interplay of these characters, with all of their frailties, Shakespeare managed to reveal his own concept of justice tempered with mercy, a justice adapted to the necessities of human beings, who must ever remain a little lower than the angels and hence not capable of that perfection of behavior demanded by purists, purists who cannot themselves live according to the stern code which they would apply to others.

SOURCE, DATE, AND HISTORY

The immediate source of *Measure for Measure* is a play by George Whetstone, published in two parts in 1578 as *Promos and Cassandra*. Whether the play was acted on any stage is uncertain. Whetstone revamped the material and published it as a tale in his collection of stories, the *Heptameron* (1582). He took his plot from a story in Giraldi Cinthio's collection of *novelle*, the *Hecatommithi* (1565). Cinthio also used the same plot in a play of his own, *Epitia*, printed in 1583. A situation somewhat like the essential plot is said to have occurred in Milan in 1547, when Fernando Gonzaga, governor of the province, left control in the hands of a deputy and pretended to disappear.

A few scholars have attempted to show that Shakespeare's play is a recast of one by another's hand, but no clear evidence supports this theory.

Others have argued that the play shows the handiwork of some collaborator, but no evidence exists for this view either, except certain passages that Shakespeare idolaters think too prosy and uninspired for him to have written.

The play was performed at Court before King James on December 26, 1604. This may have been the first performance. What sort of popular reception *Measure for Measure* had in the public playhouse we do not know, but it has kept alive over the centuries. An adaptation made by Sir William Davenant called *The Law against Lovers* was performed several times between 1661 and 1665. Another adaptation, an operatic version made by Charles Gildon, entitled *Measure for Measure, or Beauty the Best Advocate,* had a run of several years at the turn of the seventeenth century and was still being performed as late as 1706. The eighteenth century saw several revivals of *Measure for Measure* at Drury Lane and later at Covent Garden. It was revived at intervals throughout the nineteenth century and has enjoyed a number of revivals in this century. Its somewhat tortured lines and its dark plot have given this play a certain amount of acclaim in recent years from both American and English critics, who find in it expressions that appeal to their sense of the spirit of our times.

No quarto version of *Measure for Measure* was printed in the seventeenth century, and the only text is that in the First Folio of 1623. The Folio text is the basis of the present edition, with some emendations that have been generally accepted. The Folio text of this play is more corrupt and less satisfactory than many that appear in that edition.

THE AUTHOR

As early as 1598 Shakespeare was so well known as a literary and dramatic craftsman that Francis Meres, in his *Palladis Tamia: Wits Treasury*, referred in flattering terms to him as "mellifluous and honey-tongued Shakespeare," famous for his *Venus and Adonis,* his *Lucrece,* and "his sugared sonnets," which were circulating "among his private friends." Meres observes further that "as Plautus and Seneca are accounted the best for comedy and tragedy among the Latins, so Shakespeare among the English is the most excellent in both kinds for the stage," and he mentions a dozen plays that had made a name for Shakespeare. He concludes with the remark that "the Muses would speak with Shakespeare's fine filed phrase if they would speak English."

To those acquainted with the history of the Elizabethan and Jacobean periods, it is incredible that anyone should be so naïve or ignorant as to doubt the reality of Shakespeare as the author of the plays that bear his name. Yet so much nonsense has been written about other "candidates" for the plays that it is well to remind readers that no credible evidence that would stand up in a court of law has ever been adduced to prove either that Shakespeare did not write his plays or that anyone else wrote them. All the theories offered for the authorship of Francis Bacon, the Earl of Derby, the Earl of Oxford, the Earl of Hertford, Christopher Marlowe, and a score of other candidates are mere conjectures spun from the active imaginations of persons who confuse hypothesis and conjecture with evidence.

As Meres's statement of 1598 indicates, Shakespeare was already a popular playwright whose name carried weight at the box office. The obvious reputation of Shakespeare as early as 1598 makes the effort to prove him a myth one of the most absurd in the history of human perversity.

The anti-Shakespeareans talk darkly about a plot of vested interests to maintain the authorship of Shakespeare. Nobody has any vested interest in Shakespeare, but every scholar is interested in the truth and in the quality of evidence advanced by special pleaders who set forth hypotheses in place of facts.

The anti-Shakespeareans base their arguments upon a few simple premises, all of them false. These false premises are that Shakespeare was an unlettered yokel without any schooling, that nothing is known about Shakespeare, and that only a noble lord or the equivalent in background could have written the plays. The facts are that more is known about Shakespeare than about most dramatists of his day, that he had a very good education, acquired in the Stratford Grammar School, that the plays show no evidence of profound book learning, and that the knowledge of kings and courts evident in the plays is no greater than any intelligent young man could have picked up at second hand. Most anti-Shakespeareans are naïve and betray an obvious snobbery. The author of their favorite plays, they imply, must have had a college diploma framed and hung on his study wall like the one in their dentist's office, and obviously so great a writer must have had a title or some equally significant evidence of exalted social background. They forget that genius has a way of cropping up in unexpected places and that none of the great creative writers of the world got his inspiration in a college or university course.

William Shakespeare was the son of John Shakespeare of Stratford-upon-Avon, a substantial citizen of that small but busy market town in the center of the rich agricultural county of Warwick. John Shakespeare kept a shop, what we would call a general store; he dealt in wool and other produce and gradually acquired property. As a youth, John Shakespeare had learned the trade of glover and leather worker. There is no contemporary evidence that the elder Shakespeare was a butcher, though the anti-Shakespeareans like to talk about the ignorant "butcher's boy of Stratford." Their only evidence is a statement by gossipy John Aubrey, more than a century after William Shakespeare's birth, that young William followed his father's trade, and when he killed a calf, "he would do it in a high style and make a speech." We would like to believe the story true, but Aubrey is not a very credible witness.

John Shakespeare probably continued to operate a farm at Snitterfield that his father had leased. He married Mary Arden, daughter of his father's landlord, a man of some property. The third of their eight children was William, baptized on April 26, 1564, and probably born three days before. At least, it is conventional to celebrate April 23 as his birthday.

The Stratford records give considerable information about John Shakespeare. We know that he held several municipal offices including those of alderman and mayor. In 1580 he was in some sort of legal difficulty and was fined for neglecting a summons of the Court of Queen's Bench requiring him to appear at Westminster and be bound over to keep the peace.

As a citizen and alderman of Stratford, John Shakespeare was entitled to send his son to the grammar school free. Though the records are lost, there can be no reason to doubt that this is where young William received his education. As any student of the period knows, the grammar schools provided the basic education in Latin learning and literature. The Elizabethan grammar school is not to be confused with modern grammar schools. Many cultivated men of the day received all their formal education in the grammar schools. At the universities in this period a student would have received little training that would have inspired him to be a creative writer. At Stratford young Shakespeare would have acquired a familiarity with Latin and some little knowledge of Greek. He would have read Latin authors and become acquainted with the plays of Plautus and Terence. Undoubtedly, in this period of his life he received that stimulation to read and explore for himself the world of ancient and modern history which he later utilized in his plays. The youngster who does not acquire this type of intellectual curiosity *before* college days rarely develops as a result of a college course the kind of mind Shakespeare demonstrated. His learning in books was anything but profound, but he clearly had the probing curiosity that sent him in search of information, and he had a keenness in the observation of nature and of humankind that finds reflection in his poetry.

There is little documentation for Shakespeare's boyhood. There is little reason why there should be. Nobody knew that he was going to be a dramatist about whom any scrap of information would be prized in the centuries to come. He was merely an active and vigorous youth of Stratford, perhaps assisting his father in his business, and no Boswell bothered to write down facts about him. The most important record that we have is a marriage license issued by the Bishop of Worcester on November 27, 1582, to permit William Shakespeare to marry Anne Hathaway, seven or eight years his senior;

furthermore, the Bishop permitted the marriage after reading the banns only once instead of three times, evidence of the desire for haste. The need was explained on May 26, 1583, when the christening of Susanna, daughter of William and Anne Shakespeare, was recorded at Stratford. Two years later, on February 2, 1585, the records show the birth of twins to the Shakespeares, a boy and a girl who were christened Hamnet and Judith.

What William Shakespeare was doing in Stratford during the early years of his married life, or when he went to London, we do not know. It has been conjectured that he tried his hand at schoolteaching, but that is a mere guess. There is a legend that he left Stratford to escape a charge of poaching in the park of Sir Thomas Lucy of Charlecote, but there is no proof of this. There is also a legend that when first he came to London he earned his living by holding horses outside a playhouse and presently was given employment inside, but there is nothing better than eighteenth-century hearsay for this. How Shakespeare broke into the London theatres as a dramatist and actor we do not know. But lack of information is not surprising, for Elizabethans did not write their autobiographies, and we know even less about the lives of many writers and some men of affairs than we know about Shakespeare. By 1592 he was so well established and popular that he incurred the envy of the dramatist and pamphleteer Robert Greene, who referred to him as an "upstart crow . . . in his own conceit the only Shake-scene in a country." From this time onward, contemporary allusions and references in legal documents enable the scholar to chart Shakespeare's career with greater accuracy than is possible with most other Elizabethan dramatists.

By 1594 Shakespeare was a member of the company of actors known as the Lord Chamberlain's Men. After the accession of James I, in 1603, the company would have the sovereign for their patron and would be known as the King's Men. During the period of its greatest prosperity, this company would have as its principal theatres the Globe and the Blackfriars. Shakespeare was both an actor and a shareholder in the company. Tradition has assigned him such acting roles as Adam in *As You Like It* and the Ghost in *Hamlet,* a modest place on the stage that suggests that he may have had other duties in the management of the company. Such conclusions, however, are based on surmise.

What we do know is that his plays were popular and that he was highly successful in his vocation. His first play may have been *The Comedy of Errors,* acted perhaps in 1591. Certainly this was one of his earliest plays. The three parts of *Henry VI* were acted sometime between 1590 and 1592. Critics are not in agreement about precisely how much Shakespeare wrote of these three plays. *Richard III* probably dates from 1593. With this play Shakespeare captured the imagination of Elizabethan audiences, then enormously interested in historical plays. With *Richard III* Shakespeare also gave an interpretation pleasing to the Tudors of the rise to power of the grandfather of Queen Elizabeth. From this time onward, Shakespeare's plays followed on the stage in rapid succession: *Titus Andronicus, The Taming of the Shrew, The Two Gentlemen of Verona, Love's Labor's Lost, Romeo and Juliet, Richard II, A Midsummer Night's Dream, King John, The Merchant of Venice, Henry IV (Parts 1 and 2), Much Ado about Nothing, Henry V, Julius Cæsar, As You Like It, Twelfth Night, Hamlet, The Merry Wives of Windsor, All's Well That Ends Well, Measure for Measure, Othello, King Lear,* and nine others that followed before Shakespeare retired completely, about 1613.

In the course of his career in London, he made enough money to enable him to retire to Stratford with a competence. His purchase on May 4, 1597, of New Place, then the second-largest dwelling in Stratford, a "pretty house of brick and timber," with a handsome garden, indicates his increasing prosperity. There his wife and children lived while he busied himself in the London theatres. The summer before he acquired New Place, his life was darkened by the death of his only son, Hamnet, a child of eleven. In May, 1602, Shakespeare purchased one hundred and seven acres of fertile farmland near Stratford and a few months later bought a cottage and garden across the alley from New Place. About 1611, he seems to have returned permanently to Stratford, for the next year a legal document refers to him as "William Shakespeare of Stratford-upon-Avon . . . gentleman." To achieve the desired appellation of gentleman, William Shakespeare had seen to it that the College of Heralds in 1596 granted his father a coat of arms. In one step he thus became a second-generation gentleman.

Shakespeare's daughter Susanna made a good match in 1607 with Dr. John Hall, a prominent and prosperous Stratford physician. His second daughter, Judith, did not marry until she was thirty-two years old, and then, under somewhat scandalous circumstances, she married Thomas Quiney, a Stratford vintner. On March 25, 1616, Shakespeare made his will, bequeathing his landed property to Susanna, £300 to Judith, certain sums to other relatives, and his second-best bed to his wife, Anne. Much has been made of the second-best bed, but the legacy probably indicates only that Anne liked that particular bed. Shakespeare, following the practice of the time, may have already arranged with Susanna for his wife's care. Finally, on April 23, 1616, the anniversary of his birth, William Shakespeare died, and he was buried on April 25 within the chancel of Trinity Church, as befitted an honored citizen. On August 6, 1623, a few months before the publication of the collected edition of Shakespeare's plays, Anne Shakespeare joined her husband in death.

THE PUBLICATION OF HIS PLAYS

During his lifetime Shakespeare made no effort to publish any of his plays, though eighteen appeared in print in single-play editions known as quartos. Some of these are corrupt versions known as "bad quartos." No quarto, so far as is known, had the author's approval. Plays were not considered "literature" any more than most radio and television scripts today are considered literature. Dramatists sold their plays outright to the theatrical companies and it was usually considered in the company's interest to keep plays from getting into print. To achieve a reputation as a man of letters, Shakespeare wrote his *Sonnets* and his narrative poems, *Venus and Adonis* and *The Rape of Lucrece,* but he probably never dreamed that his plays would establish his reputation as a literary genius. Only Ben Jonson, a man known for his colossal conceit, had the crust to call his plays *Works,* as he did when he published an edition in 1616. But men laughed at Ben Jonson.

After Shakespeare's death, two of his old colleagues in the King's Men, John Heminges and Henry Condell, decided that it would be a good thing to print, in more accurate versions than were then available, the plays already published and eighteen additional plays not previously published in quarto. In 1623 appeared *Mr. William Shakespeares Comedies, Histories, & Tragedies. Pub-*

lished according to the True Originall Copies. London. Printed by Isaac Iaggard and Ed. Blount. This was the famous First Folio, a work that had the authority of Shakespeare's associates. The only play commonly attributed to Shakespeare that was omitted in the First Folio was *Pericles.* In their preface, "To the great Variety of Readers," Heminges and Condell state that whereas "you were abused with diverse stolen and surreptitious copies, maimed and deformed by the frauds and stealths of injurious impostors that exposed them, even those are now offered to your view cured and perfect of their limbs; and all the rest, absolute in their numbers, as he conceived them." What they used for printer's copy is one of the vexed problems of scholarship, and skilled bibliographers have devoted years of study to the question of the relation of the "copy" for the First Folio to Shakespeare's manuscripts. In some cases it is clear that the editors corrected printed quarto versions of the plays, probably by comparison with playhouse scripts. Whether these scripts were in Shakespeare's autograph is anybody's guess. No manuscript of any play in Shakespeare's handwriting has survived. Indeed, very few play manuscripts from this period by any author are extant. The Tudor and Stuart periods had not yet learned to prize autographs and authors' original manuscripts.

Since the First Folio contains eighteen plays not previously printed, it is the only source for these. For the other eighteen, which had appeared in quarto versions, the First Folio also has the authority of an edition prepared and overseen by Shakespeare's colleagues and professional associates. But since editorial standards in 1623 were far from strict, and Heminges and Condell were actors rather than editors by profession, the texts are sometimes careless. The printing and proofreading of the First Folio also left much to be desired, and some garbled passages have had to be corrected and emended. The "good quarto" texts have to be taken into account in preparing a modern edition.

Because of the great popularity of Shakespeare through the centuries, the First Folio has become a prized book, but it is not a very rare one, for it is estimated that 238 copies are extant. The Folger Shakespeare Library in Washington, D.C., has seventy-nine copies of the First Folio, collected by the founder, Henry Clay Folger, who believed that a collation of as many texts as possible would reveal significant facts about the text of Shakespeare's plays. Dr. Charlton Hinman, using an ingenious machine of his own invention for mechanical collating, has made many discoveries that throw light on Shakespeare's text and on printing practices of the day.

The probability is that the First Folio of 1623 had an edition of between 1,000 and 1,250 copies. It is believed that it sold for £1, which made it an expensive book, for £1 in 1623 was equivalent to something between $40 and $50 in modern purchasing power.

During the seventeenth century, Shakespeare was sufficiently popular to warrant three later editions in folio size, the Second Folio of 1632, the Third Folio of 1663–1664, and the Fourth Folio of 1685. The Third Folio added six other plays ascribed to Shakespeare, but these are apocryphal.

THE SHAKESPEAREAN THEATRE

The theatres in which Shakespeare's plays were performed were vastly different from those we know today. The stage was a platform that jutted out into the area now occupied by the first rows of seats on the main floor, what is called the "orchestra" in America and the "pit" in England. This platform had no curtain to come down at the ends of acts and scenes. And although simple stage properties were available, the Elizabethan theatre lacked both the machinery and the elaborate movable scenery of the modern theatre. In the rear of the platform stage was a curtained area that could be used as an inner room, a tomb, or any such scene that might be required. A balcony above this inner room, and perhaps balconies on the sides of the stage, could represent the upper deck of a ship, the entry to Juliet's room, or a prison window. A trap door in the stage provided an entrance for ghosts and devils from the nether regions, and a similar trap in the canopied structure over the stage, known as the "heavens," made it possible to let down angels on a rope. These primitive stage arrangements help to account for many elements in Elizabethan plays. For example, since there was no curtain, the dramatist frequently felt the necessity of writing into his play action to clear the stage at the ends of acts and scenes. The funeral march at the end of *Hamlet* is not there merely for atmosphere; Shakespeare had to get the corpses off the stage. The lack of scenery also freed the dramatist from undue concern about the exact location of his sets, and the physical relation of his various settings to each other did not have to be worked out with the same precision as in the modern theatre.

Before London had buildings designed exclusively for theatrical entertainment, plays were given in inns and taverns. The characteristic inn of the period had an inner courtyard with rooms opening onto balconies overlooking the yard. Players could set up their temporary stages at one end of the yard and audiences could find seats on the balconies out of the weather. The poorer sort could stand or sit on the cobblestones in the yard, which was open to the sky. The first theatres followed this construction, and throughout the Elizabethan period the large public theatres had a yard in front of the stage open to the weather, with two or three tiers of covered balconies extending around the theatre. This physical structure again influenced the writing of plays. Because a dramatist wanted the actors to be heard, he frequently wrote into his play orations that could be delivered with declamatory effect. He also provided spectacle, buffoonery, and broad jests to keep the riotous groundlings in the yard entertained and quiet.

In another respect the Elizabethan theatre differed greatly from ours. It had no actresses. All women's roles were taken by boys, sometimes recruited from the boys' choirs of the London churches. Some of these youths acted their roles with great skill and the Elizabethans did not seem to be aware of any incongruity. The first actresses on the professional English stage appeared after the Restoration of Charles II, in 1660, when exiled Englishmen brought back from France practices of the French stage.

London in the Elizabethan period, as now, was the center of theatrical interest, though wandering actors from time to time traveled through the country performing in inns, halls, and the houses of the nobility. The first professional playhouse, called simply The Theatre, was erected by James Burbage, father of Shakespeare's colleague Richard Burbage, in 1576 on lands of the old Holywell Priory adjacent to Finsbury Fields, a playground and park area just north of the city walls. It had the advantage of being outside the city's jurisdiction and yet was near enough to be easily accessible. Soon after The Theatre was opened, another playhouse called The Curtain was erected in the same neighborhood. Both of these playhouses had open courtyards and were probably polygonal in shape.

About the time The Curtain opened, Richard

Farrant, Master of the Children of the Chapel Royal at Windsor and of St. Paul's, conceived the idea of opening a "private" theatre in the old monastery buildings of the Blackfriars, not far from St. Paul's Cathedral in the heart of the city. This theatre was ostensibly to train the choirboys in plays for presentation at Court, but Farrant managed to present plays to paying audiences and achieved considerable success until aristocratic neighbors complained and had the theatre closed. This first Blackfriars Theatre was significant, however, because it popularized the boy actors in a professional way and it paved the way for a second theatre in the Blackfriars, which Shakespeare's company took over more than thirty years later. By the last years of the sixteenth century, London had at least six professional theatres and still others were erected during the reign of James I.

The Globe Theatre, the playhouse that most people connect with Shakespeare, was erected early in 1599 on the Bankside, the area across the Thames from the city. Its construction had a dramatic beginning, for on the night of December 28, 1598, James Burbage's sons, Cuthbert and Richard, gathered together a crew who tore down the old theatre in Holywell and carted the timbers across the river to a site that they had chosen for a new playhouse. The reason for this clandestine operation was a row with the landowner over the lease to the Holywell property. The site chosen for the Globe was another playground outside of the city's jurisdiction, a region of somewhat unsavory character. Not far away was the Bear Garden, an amphitheatre devoted to the baiting of bears and bulls. This was also the region occupied by many houses of ill fame licensed by the Bishop of Winchester and the source of substantial revenue to him. But it was easily accessible either from London Bridge or by means of the cheap boats operated by the London watermen, and it had the great advantage of being beyond the authority of the Puritanical aldermen of London, who frowned on plays because they lured apprentices from work, filled their heads with improper ideas, and generally exerted a bad influence. The aldermen also complained that the crowds drawn together in the theatre helped to spread the plague.

The Globe was the handsomest theatre up to its time. It was a large building, apparently octagonal in shape, and open like its predecessors to the sky in the center, but capable of seating a large audience in its covered balconies. To erect and operate the Globe, the Burbages organized a syndicate composed of the leading members of the dramatic company, of which Shakespeare was a member. Since it was open to the weather and depended on natural light, plays had to be given in the afternoon. This caused no hardship in the long afternoons of an English summer, but in the winter the weather was a great handicap and discouraged all except the hardiest. For that reason, in 1608 Shakespeare's company was glad to take over the lease of the second Blackfriars Theatre, a substantial, roomy hall reconstructed within the framework of the old monastery building. This theatre was protected from the weather and its stage was artificially lighted by chandeliers of candles. This became the winter playhouse for Shakespeare's company and at once proved so popular that the congestion of traffic created an embarrassing problem. Stringent regulations had to be made for the movement of coaches in the vicinity. Shakespeare's company continued to use the Globe during the summer months. In 1613 a squib fired from a cannon during a performance of *Henry VIII* fell on the thatched roof and the Globe burned to the ground. The next year it was rebuilt.

London had other famous theatres. The Rose, just west of the Globe, was built by Philip Henslowe, a semiliterate denizen of the Bankside, who became one of the most important theatrical owners and producers of the Tudor and Stuart periods. What is more important for historians, he kept a detailed account book, which provides much of our information about theatrical history in his time. Another famous theatre on the Bankside was the Swan, which a Dutch priest, Johannes de Witt, visited in 1596. The crude drawing of the stage which he made was copied by his friend Arend van Buchell; it is one of the important pieces of contemporary evidence for theatrical construction. Among the other theatres, the Fortune, north of the city, on Golding Lane, and the Red Bull, even farther away from the city, off St. John's Street, were the most popular. The Red Bull, much frequented by apprentices, favored sensational and sometimes rowdy plays.

The actors who kept all of these theatres going were organized into companies under the protection of some noble patron. Traditionally actors had enjoyed a low reputation. In some of the ordinances they were classed as vagrants; in the phraseology of the time, "rogues, vagabonds, sturdy beggars, and common players" were all listed together as undesirables. To escape penalties often meted out to these characters, organized groups of actors managed to gain the protection of various personages of high degree. In the later years of Elizabeth's reign, a group flourished under the name of the Queen's Men; another group had the protection of the Lord Admiral and were known as the Lord Admiral's Men. Edward Alleyn, son-in-law of Philip Henslowe, was the leading spirit in the Lord Admiral's Men. Besides the adult companies, troupes of boy actors from time to time also enjoyed considerable popularity. Among these were the Children of Paul's and the Children of the Chapel Royal.

The company with which Shakespeare had a long association had for its first patron Henry Carey, Lord Hunsdon, the Lord Chamberlain, and hence they were known as the Lord Chamberlain's Men. After the accession of James I, they became the King's Men. This company was the great rival of the Lord Admiral's Men, managed by Henslowe and Alleyn.

All was not easy for the players in Shakespeare's time, for the aldermen of London were always eager for an excuse to close up the Blackfriars and any other theatres in their jurisdiction. The theatres outside the jurisdiction of London were not immune from interference, for they might be shut up by order of the Privy Council for meddling in politics or for various other offenses, or they might be closed in time of plague lest they spread infection. During plague times, the actors usually went on tour and played the provinces wherever they could find an audience. Particularly frightening were the plagues of 1592–1594 and 1613 when the theatres closed and the players, like many other Londoners, had to take to the country.

Though players had a low social status, they enjoyed great popularity, and one of the favorite forms of entertainment at Court was the performance of plays. To be commanded to perform at Court conferred great prestige upon a company of players, and printers frequently noted that fact when they published plays. Several of Shakespeare's plays were performed before the sovereign, and Shakespeare himself undoubtedly acted in some of these plays.

REFERENCES FOR FURTHER READING

Many readers will want suggestions for further reading about Shakespeare and his times. A few references will serve as guides to further study in the enormous literature on the subject. A simple and useful little book is Gerald Sanders, *A Shakespeare Primer* (New York, 1950). *A Companion to Shakespeare Studies,* edited by Harley Granville-Barker and G. B. Harrison (Cambridge, 1934) is a valuable guide. The most recent concise handbook of facts about Shakespeare is Gerald E. Bentley, *Shakespeare: A Biographical Handbook* (New Haven, 1961). More detailed but not so voluminous as to be confusing is Hazelton Spencer, *The Art and Life of William Shakespeare* (New York, 1940), which, like Sanders' and Bentley's handbooks, contains a brief annotated list of useful books on various aspects of the subject. The most detailed and scholarly work providing complete factual information about Shakespeare is Sir Edmund Chambers, *William Shakespeare: A Study of Facts and Problems* (2 vols., Oxford, 1930).

Among other biographies of Shakespeare, Joseph Quincy Adams, *A Life of William Shakespeare* (Boston, 1923) is still an excellent assessment of the essential facts and the traditional information, and Marchette Chute, *Shakespeare of London* (New York, 1949; paperback, 1957) stresses Shakespeare's life in the theatre.

The Shakespeare Quarterly, published by the Shakespeare Association of America under the editorship of James G. McManaway, is recommended for those who wish to keep up with current Shakespearean scholarship and stage productions. The *Quarterly* includes an annual bibliography of Shakespeare editions and works on Shakespeare published during the previous year.

Two new biographies of Shakespeare have recently appeared. A. L. Rowse, *William Shakespeare: A Biography* (London, 1963; New York, 1964) provides an appraisal by a distinguished English historian, who dismisses the notion that somebody else wrote Shakespeare's plays as arrant nonsense that runs counter to known historical fact. Peter Quennell, *Shakespeare: A Biography* (Cleveland and New York, 1963) is a sensitive and intelligent survey of what is known and surmised of Shakespeare's life.

The question of the authenticity of Shakespeare's plays arouses perennial attention. The theory of hidden cryptograms in the plays is demolished by William F. and Elizebeth S. Friedman, *The Shakespearean Ciphers Examined* (New York, 1957). A succinct account of the various absurdities advanced to suggest the authorship of a multitude of candidates other than Shakespeare will be found in R. C. Churchill, *Shakespeare and His Betters* (Bloomington, Ind., 1959). Another recent discussion of the subject, *The Authorship of Shakespeare*, by James G. McManaway (Washington, D.C., 1962), presents the evidence from contemporary records to prove the identity of Shakespeare the actor-playwright with Shakespeare of Stratford.

Scholars are not in agreement about the details of playhouse construction in the Elizabethan period. John C. Adams presents a plausible reconstruction of the Globe in *The Globe Playhouse: Its Design and Equipment* (Cambridge, Mass., 1942; 2nd rev. ed., 1961). A description with excellent drawings based on Dr. Adams' model is Irwin Smith, *Shakespeare's Globe Playhouse: A Modern Reconstruction in Text and Scale Drawings* (New York, 1956). Other sensible discussions are C. Walter Hodges, *The Globe Restored* (London, 1953) and A. M. Nagler, *Shakespeare's Stage* (New Haven, 1958). Bernard Beckerman, *Shakespeare at the Globe, 1599–1609* (New Haven, 1962; paperback, 1962) discusses Elizabethan staging and acting techniques.

A sound and readable history of the early theatres is Joseph Quincy Adams, *Shakespearean Playhouses: A History of English Theatres from the Beginnings to the Restoration* (Boston, 1917). For detailed, factual information about the Elizabethan and seventeenth-century stages, the definitive reference works are Sir Edmund Chambers, *The Elizabethan Stage* (4 vols., Oxford, 1923) and Gerald E. Bentley, *The Jacobean and Caroline Stages* (5 vols., Oxford, 1941-1956).

Further information on the history of the theatre and related topics will be found in the following titles: T. W. Baldwin, *The Organization and Personnel of the Shakespearean Company* (Princeton,

1927); Lily Bess Campbell, *Scenes and Machines on the English Stage during the Renaissance* (Cambridge, 1923); Esther Cloudman Dunn, *Shakespeare in America* (New York, 1939); George C. D. Odell, *Shakespeare from Betterton to Irving* (2 vols., London, 1931); Arthur Colby Sprague, *Shakespeare and the Actors: The Stage Business in His Plays (1660-1905)* (Cambridge, Mass., 1944) and *Shakespearian Players and Performances* (Cambridge, Mass., 1953); Leslie Hotson, *The Commonwealth and Restoration Stage* (Cambridge, Mass., 1928); Alwin Thaler, *Shakspere to Sheridan: A Book about the Theatre of Yesterday and To-day* (Cambridge, Mass., 1922); George C. Branam, *Eighteenth-Century Adaptations of Shakespeare's Tragedies* (Berkeley, 1956); C. Beecher Hogan, *Shakespeare in the Theatre, 1701-1800* (Oxford, 1957); Ernest Bradlee Watson, *Sheridan to Robertson: A Study of the 19th-Century London Stage* (Cambridge, Mass., 1926); and Enid Welsford, *The Court Masque* (Cambridge, Mass., 1927).

A brief account of the growth of Shakespeare's reputation is F. E. Halliday, *The Cult of Shakespeare* (London, 1947). A more detailed discussion is given in Augustus Ralli, *A History of Shakespearian Criticism* (2 vols., Oxford, 1932; New York, 1958). Harley Granville-Barker, *Prefaces to Shakespeare* (5 vols., London, 1927-1948; 2 vols., London, 1958) provides stimulating critical discussion of the plays. An older classic of criticism is Andrew C. Bradley, *Shakespearean Tragedy: Lectures on Ham-*

let, *Othello, King Lear, Macbeth* (London, 1904; paperback, 1955). Sir Edmund Chambers, *Shakespeare: A Survey* (London, 1935; paperback, 1958) contains short, sensible essays on thirty-four of the plays, originally written as introductions to single-play editions.

For the history plays see Lily Bess Campbell, *Shakespeare's "Histories": Mirrors of Elizabethan Policy* (Cambridge, 1947); John Palmer, *Political Characters of Shakespeare* (London, 1945; 1961); E. M. W. Tillyard, *Shakespeare's History Plays* (London, 1948); Irving Ribner, *The English History Play in the Age of Shakespeare* (Princeton, 1947); and Max M. Reese, *The Cease of Majesty* (London, 1961).

The comedies are illuminated by the following studies: C. L. Barber, *Shakespeare's Festive Comedy* (Princeton, 1959); John Russell Brown, *Shakespeare and His Comedies* (London, 1957); H. B. Charlton, *Shakespearian Comedy* (London, 1938; 4th ed., 1949); W. W. Lawrence, *Shakespeare's Problem Comedies* (New York, 1931); and Thomas M. Parrott, *Shakespearean Comedy* (New York, 1949).

Measure for Measure has stimulated a considerable body of critical literature. A recent study that sums up much that has been written on the subject is Ernest Schanzer, *The Problem Plays of Shakespeare* (London, 1963). Older but still valuable for its good sense is William W. Lawrence, *Shakespeare's Problem Comedies* (New York, 1931). The play is discussed in great detail by Mary Lascelles, *Shakespeare's Measure for Measure* (London, 1953). Everyone should read for the sheer pleasure of its style R. W. Chambers, "The Jacobean Shakespeare and *Measure for Measure*." Annual Lecture of the British Academy (London, 1937). E. M. W. Tillyard, *Shakespeare's Problem Plays* (London, 1950) is succinct and sensible. Roland M. Frye, *Shakespeare and Christian Doctrine* (Princeton, 1963) provides a useful warning against a recent tendency to interpret *Measure for Measure* in terms of Christian allegory.

Further discussion of Shakespeare's tragedies, in addition to Bradley, already cited, are contained in H. B. Charlton, *Shakespearian Tragedy* (Cambridge, 1948); Willard Farnham, *The Medieval Heritage of Elizabethan Tragedy* (Berkeley, 1936) and *Shakespeare's Tragic Frontier: The World of His Final Tragedies* (Berkeley, 1950); and Harold S. Wilson, *On the Design of Shakespearian Tragedy* (Toronto, 1957).

The "Roman" plays are treated in M. M. MacCallum, *Shakespeare's Roman Plays and Their Background* (London, 1910) and J. C. Maxwell, "Shakespeare's Roman Plays, 1900-1956," *Shakespeare Survey 10* (Cambridge, 1947), 1-11.

Kenneth Muir, *Shakespeare's Sources: Comedies and Tragedies* (London, 1947) discusses Shakespeare's use of source material. The sources themselves have been reprinted several times. Among old editions are John P. Collier (ed.), *Shakespeare's Li-*

brary (2 vols., London, 1850), Israel C. Gollancz (ed.), *The Shakespeare Classics* (12 vols., London, 1907-26), and W. C. Hazlitt (ed.), *Shakespeare's Library* (6 vols., London, 1875). A modern edition is being prepared by Geoffrey Bullough with the title *Narrative and Dramatic Sources of Shakespeare* (London and New York, 1957-). Four volumes, covering the sources for the comedies and histories, have been published to date (1963).

In addition to the second edition of *Webster's New International Dictionary*, which contains most of the unusual words used by Shakespeare, the following reference works are helpful: Edwin A. Abbott, *A Shakespearian Grammar* (London, 1872); C. T. Onions, *A Shakespeare Glossary* (2nd rev. ed., Oxford, 1925); and Eric Partridge, *Shakespeare's Bawdy* (New York, 1948; paperback, 1960).

Some knowledge of the social background of the period in which Shakespeare lived is important for a full understanding of his work. A brief, clear, and accurate account of Tudor history is S. T. Bindoff, *The Tudors*, in the Penguin series. A readable general history is G. M. Trevelyan, *The History of England*, first published in 1926 and available in numerous editions. The same author's *English Social History*, first published in 1942 and also available in many editions, provides fascinating information about England in all periods. Sir John Neale, *Queen Elizabeth* (London, 1935; paperback, 1957) is the best study of the great Queen. Various aspects of life in the Elizabethan period are treated in Louis

B. Wright, *Middle-Class Culture in Elizabethan England* (Chapel Hill, N.C., 1935; reprinted Ithaca, N.Y., 1958). *Shakespeare's England: An Account of the Life and Manners of His Age,* edited by Sidney Lee and C. T. Onions (2 vols., Oxford, 1917), provides much information on many aspects of Elizabethan life. A fascinating survey of the period will be found in Muriel St. C. Byrne, *Elizabethan Life in Town and Country* (London, 1925; rev. ed., 1954; paperback, 1961).

The Folger Library is issuing a series of illustrated booklets entitled, "Folger Booklets on Tudor and Stuart Civilization," printed and distributed by Cornell University Press. Published to date are the following:

D. W. Davies, *Dutch Influences on English Culture, 1558-1625*

Giles E. Dawson, *The Life of William Shakespeare*

Ellen C. Eyler, *Early English Gardens and Garden Books*

John R. Hale, *The Art of War and Renaissance England*

William Haller, *Elizabeth I and the Puritans*

Virginia A. LaMar, *English Dress in the Age of Shakespeare*

————, *Travel and Roads in England*

John L. Lievsay, *The Elizabethan Image of Italy*

James G. McManaway, *The Authorship of Shake-speare*

Dorothy E. Mason, *Music in Elizabethan England*

Garrett Mattingly, *The "Invincible" Armada and Elizabethan England*

Boies Penrose, *Tudor and Early Stuart Voyaging*

Conyers Read, *The Government of England under Elizabeth*

Albert J. Schmidt, *The Yeoman in Tudor and Stuart England*

Lilly C. Stone, *English Sports and Recreations*

Craig R. Thompson, *The Bible in English, 1525-1611*

————, *The English Church in the Sixteenth Century*

————, *Schools in Tudor England*

————, *Universities in Tudor England*

At intervals the Folger Library plans to gather these booklets in hardbound volumes. The first is *Life and Letters in Tudor and Stuart England, First Folger Series*, edited by Louis B. Wright and Virginia A. LaMar (published for the Folger Shakespeare Library by Cornell University Press, 1962). The volume contains eleven of the booklets.

The Names of All the Actors

Vincentio, the Duke.
Angelo, the deputy.
Escalus, an ancient lord.
Claudio, a young gentleman.
Lucio, a fantastic.
Two other like gentlemen.
Provost.
Thomas, } two friars.
Peter, }
[A Justice.]
[*Varrius*.]
Elbow, a simple constable.
Froth, a foolish gentleman.
[*Pompey*, the clown, servant to *Mistress Overdone*.]
Abhorson, an executioner.
Barnardine, a dissolute prisoner.
Isabella, sister to *Claudio*.
Mariana, betrothed to *Angelo*.
Juliet, beloved of *Claudio*.
Francisca, a nun.
Mistress Overdone, a bawd.

[Lords, Officers, Citizens, Boy, and Attendants.]

SCENE: Vienna.

MEASURE
FOR
MEASURE

ACT I

I.i. Duke Vincentio, ruler of Vienna, reveals to Lord Escalus his plan to leave the government of the city in the hands of Lord Angelo, with Escalus as his assistant, while he himself leaves Vienna. Angelo is modestly reluctant to assume the responsibility, but the Duke insists that Angelo's virtues qualify him to rule with full power.

━━━━━━━━━━━━━━━━━

3–9. Of government . . . work: evidently a line, or part of one, has been lost in this passage, since the phrasing seems cryptic and elliptical even for this play, which has many cryptic passages. The sense may be paraphrased: "For me to describe the characteristics of government would be mere oratory, since I am aware that your knowledge of the subject surpasses my ability to advise you. I need only give you the necessary authority and leave you to exercise it in accordance with your abilities."

5. science: knowledge.

6. lists: limits.

8. sufficiency: competence.

11. pregnant in: versed in; full of.

12. art and practice: knowledge and experience.

14. warp: deviate.

16. What figure of us think you he will bear: how do you think he will conduct himself in my place?

17. with special soul: with complete confidence.

ACT I

Scene I. [An apartment in the Duke's palace.]

Enter Duke, Escalus, Lords [and Attendants].

Duke. Escalus.
Escal. My lord.
Duke. Of government the properties to unfold
Would seem in me t' affect speech and discourse;
Since I am put to know that your own science   5
Exceeds, in that, the lists of all advice
My strength can give you: then no more remains
But that to your sufficiency, as your worth is able,
And let them work. The nature of our people,
Our city's institutions, and the terms   10
For common justice y'are as pregnant in
As art and practice hath enriched any
That we remember. There is our commission,
From which we would not have you warp. Call hither,
I say, bid come before us Angelo.   15
                    [*Exit an Attendant.*]
What figure of us think you he will bear?
For you must know, we have with special soul

I

18. **Elected:** chosen; **our absence to supply:** to replace me in my absence.

20. **organs:** administrative instruments.

29. **character in thy life:** symbolism in thy habitual conduct.

31. **belongings:** endowments of character.

32. **proper:** exclusively. The word usually emphasizes personal ownership.

34–35. **Heaven doth with us as we with torches do,/Not light them for themselves:** an echo of the biblical passage: "Neither do men light a candle and put it under a bushel, but on a candlestick and it giveth light unto all that are in the house. Let your light to shine before men, that they may see your good works and glorify your father which is in Heaven" (Matt. 5:15-6).

38. **but to fine issues:** except for the purpose of achieving fine deeds.

40. **determines:** ensures.

42. **use:** interest; profit.

43. **my part in him advertise:** i.e., can instruct himself how to perform my role.

44. **Hold:** remain true (to the character that the Duke attributes to him).

Elected him our absence to supply,
Lent him our terror, dressed him with our love,
And given his deputation all the organs   20
Of our own power: what think you of it?
   Escal. If any in Vienna be of worth
To undergo such ample grace and honor,
It is Lord Angelo.

Enter Angelo.

   Duke.   Look where he comes.   25
   Ang. Always obedient to your Grace's will,
I come to know your pleasure.
   Duke.   Angelo,
There is a kind of character in thy life
That to the observer doth thy history   30
Fully unfold. Thyself and thy belongings
Are not thine own so proper as to waste
Thyself upon thy virtues, they on thee.
Heaven doth with us as we with torches do,
Not light them for themselves; for if our virtues   35
Did not go forth of us, 'twere all alike
As if we had them not. Spirits are not finely touched
But to fine issues; nor Nature never lends
The smallest scruple of her excellence
But, like a thrifty goddess, she determines   40
Herself the glory of a creditor,
Both thanks and use. But I do bend my speech
To one that can my part in him advertise;
Hold therefore, Angelo.

45. **remove**: absence; **at full ourself**: endowed with my full authority.

48. **first in question**: first considered; senior.

51. **mettle**: spirit, with a pun on "metal."

55. **leavened**: thoroughly considered.

57. **of so quick condition**: so urgent.

58. **prefers itself**: recommends its own priority; **unquestioned**: unconsidered.

60. **importune**: necessitate.

66. **bring**: escort; **something**: somewhat.

70. **qualify**: moderate.

73. **stage**: display (as on a stage).

In our remove be thou at full ourself;   45
Mortality and mercy in Vienna
Live in thy tongue and heart. Old Escalus,
Though first in question, is thy secondary.
Take thy commission.

    Ang.   Now, good my lord,   50
Let there be some more test made of my mettle,
Before so noble and so great a figure
Be stamped upon it.

    Duke.   No more evasion:
We have with a leavened and prepared choice   55
Proceeded to you; therefore take your honors.
Our haste from hence is of so quick condition
That it prefers itself and leaves unquestioned
Matters of needful value. We shall write to you,
As time and our concernings shall importune,   60
How it goes with us; and do look to know
What doth befall you here. So fare you well.
To the hopeful execution do I leave you
Of your commissions.

    Ang.   Yet give leave, my lord,   65
That we may bring you something on the way.

    Duke. My haste may not admit it;
Nor need you, on mine honor, have to do
With any scruple: your scope is as mine own,
So to enforce or qualify the laws   70
As to your soul seems good. Give me your hand.
I'll privily away. I love the people
But do not like to stage me to their eyes.
Though it do well, I do not relish well

75. **aves:** greetings.
77. **affect it:** enjoy popularity.
89. **wait upon:** accompany.

***

I.ii. Lucio, a frivolous man-about-town and friend of Claudio, learns from Mistress Overdone, a brothel-keeper, that Claudio has been arrested for getting his betrothed, Juliet, with child. Claudio and Juliet come by in the custody of the provost and officers, and Claudio explains that he and Juliet had contracted marriage but delayed legal confirmation because of an insufficient dowry. Lord Angelo, who has begun to enforce a neglected statute against fornication, threatens Claudio with the death penalty for its infringement. Lucio advises his friend to send after Duke Vincentio and appeal to him. Claudio, unable to find the Duke, asks Lucio to seek his (Claudio's) sister at a cloister which she is about to enter and ask her to appeal to the Duke's deputy. Lucio promises to do so.

***

2. **composition:** agreement.

Their loud applause and aves vehement;   75
Nor do I think the man of safe discretion
That does affect it. Once more, fare you well.
  Ang. The Heavens give safety to your purposes.
  Escal. Lead forth and bring you back in happiness!
  Duke. I thank you. Fare you well.   *Exit.*   80
  Escal. I shall desire you, sir, to give me leave
To have free speech with you; and it concerns me
To look into the bottom of my place.
A pow'r I have, but of what strength and nature
I am not yet instructed.   85
  Ang. 'Tis so with me. Let us withdraw together,
And we may soon our satisfaction have
Touching that point.
  Escal.   I'll wait upon your Honor.
                          Exeunt.

Scene II. [A street.]

Enter Lucio and two other Gentlemen.

  Lucio. If the Duke, with the other dukes, come not
to composition with the King of Hungary, why then
all the dukes fall upon the King.
  1. Gent. Heaven grant us its peace, but not the
King of Hungary's!   5
  2. Gent. Amen.
  Lucio. Thou concludest like the sanctimonious pi-

27–28. **there went but a pair of shears between us:** "we are made of the same stuff," a proverbial saying.

29. **lists:** selvage.

32. **three-piled:** of triple thickness.

33. **kersey:** coarse woolen cloth.

34. **French velvet:** a reference to "French disease" (syphilis). **Piled** signifies "peeled" (bald) from loss of hair due to the disease.

34–35. **feelingly:** i.e., so as to make an impression on you; "have I scored a hit?"

37. **painful feeling:** Lucio implies that the gentleman has mouth sores, another result of syphilis.

rate, that went to sea with the Ten Commandments
but scraped one out of the table.

2. Gent. "Thou shalt not steal"?   10

Lucio. Ay, that he razed.

1. Gent. Why, 'twas a commandment to command
the captain and all the rest from their functions: they
put forth to steal. There's not a soldier of us all that
in the thanksgiving before meat do relish the peti-   15
tion well that prays for peace.

2. Gent. I never heard any soldier dislike it.

Lucio. I believe thee; for I think thou never wast
where grace was said.

2. Gent. No? A dozen times at least.   20

1. Gent. What, in meter?

Lucio. In any proportion or in any language.

1. Gent. I think, or in any religion.

Lucio. Ay, why not? Grace is grace, despite of all
controversy: as, for example, thou thyself art a   25
wicked villain, despite of all grace.

1. Gent. Well, there went but a pair of shears between us.

Lucio. I grant; as there may between the lists and
the velvet. Thou art the list.   30

1. Gent. And thou the velvet: thou art good velvet; thou'rt a three-piled piece, I warrant thee. I had
as lief be a list of an English kersey as be piled, as
thou art piled, for a French velvet. Do I speak feelingly now?   35

Lucio. I think thou dost; and, indeed, with most
painful feeling of thy speech. I will, out of thine own

*unmerited.
favor*

38. **begin:** i.e., toast.

39. **forget to drink after thee:** i.e., have a care not to take his infection by drinking from the same vessel.

40. **done myself wrong:** exposed myself to ridicule.

49. **dolors:** afflictions, with a pun on "dollars."

51. **French crown:** pun on the coin and a bald pate from the French disease.

confession, learn to begin thy health, but, whilst I
live, forget to drink after thee.

1. Gent. I think I have done myself wrong, have I   40
not?

2. Gent. Yes, that thou hast, whether thou art tainted or free.

Enter Bawd [Mistress Overdone].

Lucio. Behold, behold, where Madam Mitigation
comes! I have purchased as many diseases under her   45
roof as come to—

2. Gent. To what, I pray?

Lucio. Judge.

2. Gent. To three thousand dolors a year.

1. Gent. Ay, and more.   50

Lucio. A French crown more.

1. Gent. Thou art always figuring diseases in me;
but thou art full of error: I am sound.

Lucio. Nay, not, as one would say, healthy; but so
sound as things that are hollow. Thy bones are hol-   55
low; impiety has made a feast of thee.

1. Gent. [*To Mistress Overdone*] How now! which
of your hips has the most profound sciatica?

Mrs. Over. Well, well; there's one yonder arrested
and carried to prison was worth five thousand of you   60
all.

2. Gent. Who's that, I pray thee?

Mrs. Over. Marry, sir, that's Claudio, Signior
Claudio.

82. **sweat:** plague.
83. **custom-shrunk:** i.e., business is bad.
89. **peculiar:** private.

DEATH steals overdones
Mistress overdones
Customers

1. Gent. Claudio to prison? 'Tis not so.   65

Mrs. Over. Nay, but I know 'tis so: I saw him arrested; saw him carried away; and, which is more, within these three days his head to be chopped off.

Lucio. But, after all this fooling, I would not have it so. Art thou sure of this?   70

Mrs. Over. I am too sure of it; and it is for getting Madam Julietta with child.

Lucio. Believe me, this may be: he promised to meet me two hours since, and he was ever precise in promise-keeping.   75

2. Gent. Besides, you know, it draws something near to the speech we had to such a purpose.

1. Gent. But, most of all, agreeing with the proclamation.

Lucio. Away! let's go learn the truth of it.   80
                    Exeunt [*Lucio and Gentlemen*].

Mrs. Over. Thus, what with the war, what with the sweat, what with the gallows, and what with poverty, I am custom-shrunk.

Enter Clown [*Pompey*].

How now! what's the news with you?

Pom. Yonder man is carried to prison.   85

Mrs. Over. Well, what has he done?

Pom. A woman.

Mrs. Over. But what's his offense?

Pom. Groping for trouts in a peculiar river.

Fisher of menses

95. **houses:** brothels, which were usually located in the suburbs of London to avoid the jurisdiction of city magistrates.

112. **Thomas Tapster:** a conventional nickname for all tapsters.

Mrs. Over. What, is there a maid with child by 90 him?

Pom. No, but there's a woman with maid by him. You have not heard of the proclamation, have you?

Mrs. Over. What proclamation, man?

Pom. All houses in the suburbs of Vienna must be 95 plucked down.

Mrs. Over. And what shall become of those in the city?

Pom. They shall stand for seed; they had gone down too but that a wise burgher put in for them. 100

Mrs. Over. But shall all our houses of resort in the suburbs be pulled down?

Pom. To the ground, mistress.

Mrs. Over. Why, here's a change indeed in the commonwealth! What shall become of me? 105

Pom. Come, fear not you: good counselors lack no clients. Though you change your place, you need not change your trade: I'll be your tapster still. Courage! there will be pity taken on you: you that have worn your eyes almost out in the service, you will be con- 110 sidered.

Mrs. Over. What's to do here, Thomas Tapster? Let's withdraw.

Pom. Here comes Signior Claudio, led by the provost to prison; and there's Madam Juliet. *Exeunt.* 115

Enter Provost, Claudio, Juliet, and Officers, [followed by] Lucio and two Gentlemen.

123–24. **The words of Heaven: on whom it will, it will;/On whom it will not, so:** referring to Romans 9:15: "I will have mercy on whom I will have mercy, and I will have compassion on whom I will have compassion." Claudio comments bitterly that human authority can apply the full rigor of the law as though it were as immune from question as Heaven itself.

129. **scope:** freedom.

130–32. **Our natures do pursue,/Like rats that ravin down their proper bane,/A thirsty evil; and when we drink, we die:** i.e., we each indulge the vice that will prove most fatal to us and thus bring about our own deaths; **ravin:** gulp ravenously; **proper bane:** personal poison; **thirsty:** thirst-provoking.

135–36. **I had as lief have the foppery of freedom as the morality of imprisonment:** I would just as soon be foolish and free as a prisoner wise enough to moralize on his predicament; **foppery:** foolishness.

   Claud. Fellow, why dost thou show me thus to the
     world?
Bear me to prison, where I am committed.
   Pro. I do it not in evil disposition,
But from Lord Angelo by special charge.   120
   Claud. Thus can the demigod Authority
Make us pay down for our offense by weight
The words of Heaven: on whom it will, it will;
On whom it will not, so. Yet still 'tis just.
   Lucio. Why, how now, Claudio! whence comes this 125
restraint?
   Claud. From too much liberty, my Lucio, liberty.
As surfeit is the father of much fast,
So every scope by the immoderate use
Turns to restraint. Our natures do pursue,   130
Like rats that ravin down their proper bane,
A thirsty evil; and when we drink, we die.
   Lucio. If I could speak so wisely under an arrest, I
would send for certain of my creditors; and yet, to
say the truth, I had as lief have the foppery of free- 135
dom as the morality of imprisonment. What's thy
offense, Claudio?
   Claud. What but to speak of would offend again.
   Lucio. What, is't murder?
   Claud. No.   140
   Lucio. Lechery?
   Claud. Call it so.
   Pro. Away, sir! you must go.
   Claud. One word, good friend—Lucio, a word with
you.   145

147. **looked after:** i.e., given importance.

148. **true contract:** pre-contract, consisting of a mutual verbal promise to marry. Such an espousal was considered legally binding, but the church forbade consummation before the performance of the religious rites.

150. **fast:** securely.

151–52. **denunciation . . ./Of outward order:** i.e., the saying of the banns and the church ceremony.

153. **propagation:** i.e., hope of increasing.

155. **meet:** appropriate.

156. **made them for us:** brought them to favor the match.

158. **gross:** evident; great.

162. **Fault and glimpse of newness:** i.e., the faulty perception of a novice (Angelo).

166. **straight:** immediately.

169. **I stagger in:** I am uncertain.

170. **Awakes me:** awakes (the ethical dative construction).

172. **zodiacs:** years. The Duke says in the next scene (line 22) that the period has been fourteen years.

173. **for a name:** to enhance his own reputation.

Lucio. A hundred, if they'll do you any good.
Is lechery so looked after?

Claud. Thus stands it with me: upon a true contract
I got possession of Julietta's bed.
You know the lady: she is <u>fast</u> my wife,   150
Save that we do the denunciation lack
Of outward order. This we came not to
Only for propagation of a dow'r
Remaining in the coffer of her friends,
From whom we thought it meet to hide our love   155
Till time had made them for us. But it chances
The stealth of our most mutual entertainment
With character too gross is writ on Juliet.

Lucio. With child, perhaps?

Claud.   Unhappily, even so.   160
And the new deputy now for the Duke—
Whether it be the fault and glimpse of newness,
Or whether that the body public be
A horse whereon the governor doth ride,
Who, newly in the seat, that it may know   165
He can command lets it straight feel the spur;
Whether the tyranny be in his place,
Or in his eminence that fills it up,
I stagger in—but this new governor
Awakes me all the enrolled penalties   170
Which have, like unscoured armor, hung by the wall
So long that nineteen zodiacs have gone round
And none of them been worn; and, for a name,
Now puts the drowsy and neglected act
Freshly on me. 'Tis surely for a name.   175

176. **tickle:** insecure.

183. **approbation:** probation; acceptance as a novice of the order.

185. **in my voice:** on my behalf.

188. **prone:** tempting; that is, an appeal made without words.

Lucio. I warrant it is; and thy head stands so tickle
on thy shoulders that a milkmaid, if she be in love,
may sigh it off. Send after the Duke and appeal to
him.

Claud. I have done so, but he's not to be found. 180
I prithee, Lucio, do me this kind service:
This day my sister should the cloister enter
And there receive her approbation.
Acquaint her with the danger of my state;
Implore her, in my voice, that she make friends 185
To the strict deputy. Bid herself <u>assay</u> him.
I have great hope in that; for in her youth
There is a prone and speechless dialect
Such as move men; beside, she hath prosperous art
When she will play with reason and discourse, 190
And well she can persuade.

Lucio. I pray she may; as well for the encouragement of the like, which else would stand under griev-
ous imposition, as for the enjoying of thy life, who I
would be sorry should be thus foolishly lost at a game 195
of tick-tack. I'll to her.

Claud. I thank you, good friend Lucio.

Lucio. Within two hours.

Claud.   Come, officer, away!

Exeunt.

I.[iii.] The Duke, having assumed the habit and identity of a friar, explains to Friar Thomas the reason for his pretended departure from Vienna and the selection of Lord Angelo to rule in his place. For some time he has allowed the city's laws to go unenforced. He now feels he would receive criticism if he himself chastised the people for a laxity he has so long permitted. Hence, he has decided to give the authority to Angelo. He indicates that Angelo is puritanical and considers himself above human weakness; the power now in his hands may reveal his true character.

▬▬▬▬▬▬▬▬▬▬

2. **dribbling:** literally, "missing the mark"; i.e., feeble.

3. **complete bosom:** invulnerable heart.

9. **removed:** secluded.

10. **held in idle price:** had a low opinion of; **to haunt:** the haunting of.

11. **youth and cost:** extravagant youth; **bravery:** magnificence.

13. **stricture:** strictness; scrupulous morality.

23. **o'ergrown:** i.e., grown old and heavy.

12

DISCHARGE — Expense of spirit
GUILT

Scene [III. A monastery].

Enter Duke and Friar Thomas.

Duke. No, holy father, throw away that thought:
Believe not that the dribbling dart of love
Can pierce a complete bosom. Why I desire thee
To give me secret harbor hath a purpose
More grave and wrinkled than the aims and ends   5
Of burning youth.
      Friar.   May your Grace speak of it?
Duke. My holy sir, none better knows than you
How I have ever loved the life removed
And held in idle price to haunt assemblies   10
Where youth and cost a witless bravery keeps.
I have delivered to Lord Angelo,
A man of stricture and firm abstinence,
My absolute power and place here in Vienna,
And he supposes me traveled to Poland;   15
For so I have strewed it in the common ear,
And so it is received. Now, pious sir,
You will demand of me why I do this.
      Friar. Gladly, my lord.
      Duke. We have strict statutes and most biting laws,   20
The needful bits and curbs to headstrong weeds,
Which for this fourteen years we have let slip,
Even like an o'ergrown lion in a cave
That goes not out to prey. Now, as fond fathers,
Having bound up the threat'ning twigs of birch   25

30. **liberty:** license.

38. **Sith:** since.

39. **gall:** wound.

44. **strike home:** punish severely.

45–46. **my nature never in the sight/To do it slander:** i.e., since I shall not be seen as the agent, I shall be safe from criticism.

46. **sway:** rule.

50. **formally:** in the proper form; properly; **bear:** behave.

51. **Mo:** more.

52. **At our more leisure:** when I have more time.

53. **precise:** puritanical.

54. **Stands at a guard with envy:** is wary of exposing himself to malice; guards his reputation.

The "o'ergrown lion" of Aesop's fable. From Gabriele Faerno, *Fabulae C. Aesopicae* (1590).

13

Only to stick it in their children's sight
For terror, not to use, in time the rod
Becomes more mocked than feared, so our decrees,
Dead to infliction, to themselves are dead,
And liberty plucks Justice by the nose,   30
The baby beats the nurse, and quite athwart
Goes all decorum.
    Friar.   It rested in your Grace
To unloose this tied-up justice when you pleased;
And it in you more dreadful would have seemed   35
Than in Lord Angelo.
    Duke.   I do fear, too dreadful:
Sith 'twas my fault to give the people scope,
'Twould be my tyranny to strike and gall them
For what I bid them do: for we bid this be done,   40
When evil deeds have their permissive pass
And not the punishment. Therefore, indeed, my father,
I have on Angelo imposed the office;
Who may, in the ambush of my name, strike home,
And yet my nature never in the sight   45
To do it slander. And to behold his sway
I will, as 'twere a brother of your order,
Visit both prince and people: therefore, I prithee,
Supply me with the <u>habit</u> and instruct me
How I may formally in person bear   50
Like a true friar. Mo reasons for this action
At our more leisure shall I render you;
Only, this one: Lord Angelo is precise;
Stands at a guard with envy; scarce confesses
That his blood flows or that his appetite   55

I.[iv.] Lucio arrives at the nunnery where Claudio's sister, Isabella, is to take her vows. He reports that Claudio is certain to be executed for his offense unless she can persuade Angelo to relent. Isabella agrees to call upon Angelo and plead with him.

‖‖‖‖‖‖‖‖‖‖‖‖‖‖‖‖‖‖‖‖‖‖‖‖‖

18. **stead:** assist.

Is more to bread than stone. Hence shall we see,
If power change purpose, what our seemers be.

Exeunt.

Scene [IV. A nunnery].

Enter Isabella and Francisca, a nun.

Isa. And have you nuns no farther privileges?
Fran. Are not these large enough?
Isa. Yes, truly: I speak not as desiring more,
But rather wishing a more strict restraint
Upon the sisterhood, the votarists of St. Clare.   5
  Lucio. [*Within*] Ho! Peace be in this place!
Isa.   Who's that which calls?
Fran. It is a man's voice. Gentle Isabella,
Turn you the key and know his business of him.
You may; I may not. You are yet unsworn;   10
When you have vowed, you must not speak with men
But in the presence of the prioress.
Then if you speak, you must not show your face;
Or, if you show your face, you must not speak.
He calls again: I pray you, answer him.   [*Exit.*]   15
  Isa. Peace and prosperity! Who is't that calls?

[*Enter Lucio.*]

Lucio. Hail, virgin, if you be, as those cheek roses
Proclaim you are no less! Can you so stead me

25–26. kindly greets you: offers his filial greetings.

31. friend: lover; mistress.

32. make me not your story: don't make up tales for my benefit.

35. to seem the lapwing: a reference to the lapwing's trick of pretending a hurt and leading a possible enemy away from her nest.

37. hold: regard; **enskied:** divine.

42. Fewness and truth: in a few truthful words.

46. seedness: seeding; **fallow:** plowed land.

47. foison: plenty.

As bring me to the sight of Isabella,
A novice of this place and the fair sister   20
To her unhappy brother Claudio?
  Isa. Why "her unhappy brother"? Let me ask,
The rather for I now must make you know
I am that Isabella and his sister.
  Lucio. Gentle and fair, your brother kindly greets   25
    you.
Not to be weary with you, he's in prison.
  Isa. Woe me! for what?
  Lucio. For that which, if myself might be his judge,
He should receive his punishment in thanks: 30
He hath got his friend with child.
  Isa. Sir, make me not your story.
  Lucio.   It is true.
I would not—though 'tis my familiar sin
With maids to seem the lapwing and to jest,   35
Tongue far from heart—play with all virgins so:
I hold you as a thing enskied and sainted,
By your renouncement, an immortal spirit,
And to be talked with in sincerity,
As with a saint.   40
  Isa. You do blaspheme the good in mocking me.
  Lucio. Do not believe it. Fewness and truth, 'tis
    thus:
Your brother and his lover have embraced.
As those that feed grow full, as blossoming time,   45
That from the seedness the bare fallow brings
To teeming foison, even so her plenteous womb
Expresseth his full tilth and husbandry.

52. **vain:** idle.

57–58. **Bore . . ./In hand and hope of action:**
deceived . . . with the hope of action.

59. **nerves:** sinews.

60. **givings-out:** announced intentions.

62. **line:** range.

65. **motions:** impulses.

66. **rebate:** synonymous with **blunt.**

68. **use and liberty:** habitual license.

71. **heavy sense:** severe interpretation.

Illustration to Aesop's fable of the mice that play contemptuously
near a helpless cat (the "lion" of Lucio's phrase). From Gabriele
Faerno, *Fabulae C. Aesopicae* (1590).

Isa. Someone with child by him?—My cousin Juliet?

Lucio. Is she your cousin? 50

Isa. Adoptedly, as schoolmaids change their names
By vain, though apt, affection.

Lucio. She it is.

Isa. O, let him marry her.

Lucio. This is the point. 55
The Duke is very strangely gone from hence;
Bore many gentlemen, myself being one,
In hand and hope of action: but we do learn
By those that know the very nerves of state,
His givings-out were of an infinite distance 60
From his true-meant design. Upon his place,
And with full line of his authority,
Governs Lord Angelo, a man whose blood
Is very snow-broth, one who never feels
The wanton stings and motions of the sense 65
But doth rebate and blunt his natural edge
With profits of the mind, study, and fast.
He—to give fear to use and liberty,
Which have for long run by the hideous law,
As mice by lions—hath picked out an act 70
Under whose heavy sense your brother's life
Falls into forfeit. He arrests him on it
And follows close the rigor of the statute,
To make him an example. All hope is gone,
Unless you have the grace by your fair prayer 75
To soften Angelo: and that's my pith of business
'Twixt you and your poor brother.

Isa. Doth he so seek his life?

79. **censured:** passed sentence upon.

89–92. **when maidens sue,/Men give like gods; but when they weep and kneel,/All their petitions are as freely theirs/As they themselves would owe them:** when maidens petition, men may grant what they want as a favor (i.e., with condescension); but when maidens beg humbly in tears, they receive their wish as though it were their due; **owe:** own.

98. **Soon at night:** tonight.

 Lucio.   Has censured him
Already; and, as I hear, the provost hath   80
A warrant for his execution.
 Isa. Alas! what poor ability's in me
To do him good?
 Lucio.   Assay the pow'r you have.
 Isa. My power? Alas, I doubt—   85
 Lucio.   Our doubts are traitors
And makes us lose the good we oft might win
By fearing to attempt. Go to Lord Angelo
And let him learn to know, when maidens sue,
Men give like gods; but when they weep and kneel,   90
All their petitions are as freely theirs
As they themselves would owe them.
 Isa. I'll see what I can do.
 Lucio.   But speedily.
 Isa. I will about it straight,   95
No longer staying but to give the Mother
Notice of my affair. I humbly thank you.
Commend me to my brother. Soon at night
I'll send him certain word of my success.
 Lucio. I take my leave of you.   100
 Isa.   Good sir, adieu.
         Exeunt.

MEASURE
FOR
MEASURE

ACT II

II.i. Escalus tries to persuade Angelo that justice should be tempered with mercy because all humans are weak. Even he himself might conceivably commit the same sin as Claudio. Angelo, however, is confident that he would never fall. Determined that Claudio shall die, he gives orders to the provost to see that Claudio is executed by nine the following morning. Elbow, a constable, appears with two prisoners, Froth and Pompey, the latter a tapster in a brothel. Angelo and Escalus can make no sense out of the situation as Elbow tries to explain it, and Angelo finally leaves the determination of the matter to Escalus, who dismisses them all with a warning.

▪▪▪▪▪▪▪▪▪▪▪▪▪▪▪▪▪▪▪▪▪▪▪▪▪▪▪▪▪▪▪

2. **fear:** frighten.
7. **fall:** let fall.
10. **strait:** strict.

ACT II

Scene I. [A hall in Angelo's house.]

Enter Angelo, Escalus, [and a] Justice,
[Officers and other Attendants behind].

Ang. We must not make a scarecrow of the law,
Setting it up to fear the birds of prey,
And let it keep one shape, till custom make it
Their perch and not their terror.
Escal.   Ay, but yet   5
Let us be keen and rather cut a little
Than fall and bruise to death. Alas, this gentleman
Whom I would save had a most noble father!
Let but your Honor know,
Whom I believe to be most strait in virtue,   10
That, in the working of your own affections,
Had time cohered with place or place with wishing,
Or that the resolute acting of your blood
Could have attained the effect of your own purpose,
Whether you had not sometime in your life   15
Erred in this point which now you censure him
And pulled the law upon you.
Ang. 'Tis one thing to be tempted, Escalus,
Another thing to fall. I not deny,

22. **open made:** revealed.

24. **What knows the laws:** i.e., how can the law know.

25. **pregnant:** natural.

30. **For:** because.

33. **nothing come in partial:** no partiality be shown me.

36. **like:** please.

40. **pilgrimage:** term of life; man's life on earth was often likened to a pilgrimage.

44. **brakes:** thickets; i.e., a complex of sins; **answer:** pay for.

An emblematic representation of human life as a pilgrimage. From Geoffrey Whitney, *A Choice of Emblems* (1586).

The jury, passing on the prisoner's life,   20
May in the sworn twelve have a thief or two
Guiltier than him they try. What's open made to
    justice,
That justice seizes. What knows the laws
That thieves do pass on thieves? 'Tis very pregnant, 25
The jewel that we find, we stoop and take't
Because we see it; but what we do not see
We tread upon and never think of it.
You may not so extenuate his offense
For I have had such faults; but rather tell me,   30
When I, that censure him, do so offend,
Let mine own judgment pattern out my death,
And nothing come in partial. Sir, he must die.

Enter Provost.

  Escal. Be it as your wisdom will.
  Ang.   Where is the provost? 35
  Pro. Here, if it like your Honor.
  Ang.   See that Claudio
Be executed by nine tomorrow morning.
Bring him his confessor, let him be prepared;
For that's the utmost of his pilgrimage.   40
                        [Exit Provost.]
  Escal. [*Aside*] Well, Heaven forgive him! and for-
    give us all!
Some rise by sin, and some by virtue fall.
Some run from brakes of vice and answer none;
And some condemned for a fault alone.   45

52–53. poor Duke's constable: poor constable of the Duke.

59. precise: Elbow means "downright," but there is a pun on the sense "puritanical," as at I.[iii.]53.

60. profanation: reverence. Like many minor characters of Shakespeare's, Elbow uses words that mean the opposite of what he intends to say.

65. out: "at a loss for words," with a pun on the familiar phrase.

67. parcel-bawd: a part-time bawd.

70. hothouse: public bath.

Enter Elbow, Froth, Clown, [and] Officers.

Elb. Come, bring them away. If these be good people in a commonweal that do nothing but use their abuses in common houses, I know no law. Bring them away.

Ang. How now, sir! What's your name? and what's 50 the matter?

Elb. If it please your Honor, I am the poor Duke's constable and my name is Elbow. I do lean upon justice, sir, and do bring in here before your good Honor two notorious benefactors. 55

Ang. Benefactors? Well; what benefactors are they? are they not malefactors?

Elb. If it please your Honor, I know not well what they are: but precise villains they are, that I am sure of, and void of all profanation in the world that good 60 Christians ought to have.

Escal. This comes off well: here's a wise officer.

Ang. Go to; what quality are they of? Elbow *is* your name? Why dost thou not speak, Elbow?

Pom. He cannot, sir: he's out at elbow. 65

Ang. What are you, sir?

Elb. He, sir! a tapster, sir, parcel-bawd; one that serves a bad woman, whose house, sir, was, as they say, plucked down in the suburbs; and now she professes a hothouse, which, I think, is a very ill house 70 too.

Escal. How know you that?

73. **detest:** protest.

76. **honest:** respectable.

81. **naughty:** wicked.

84. **cardinally:** carnally.

90. **varlets:** menials or knaves. Elbow continues to misspeak himself; by **varlets** he means Escalus and Angelo.

94. **stewed prunes:** notorious as fare offered in brothels, because of a common belief in their virtue to prevent and relieve venereal disease.

96. **distant time:** i.e., instant.

100. **not of a pin:** i.e., not worth a pin.

Elb. My wife, sir, whom I detest before Heaven
and your Honor—

Escal. How? thy wife? 75

Elb. Ay, sir—whom, I thank Heaven, is an honest
woman—

Escal. Dost thou detest her therefore?

Elb. I say, sir, I will detest myself also, as well as
she, that this house, if it be not a bawd's house, it is 80
pity of her life, for it is a naughty house.

Escal. How dost thou know that, constable?

Elb. Marry, sir, by my wife; who, if she had been
a woman cardinally given, might have been accused
in fornication, adultery, and all uncleanliness there. 85

Escal. By the woman's means?

Elb. Ay, sir, by Mistress Overdone's means: but, as
she spit in his face, so she defied him.

Pom. Sir, if it please your Honor, this is not so.

Elb. Prove it before these varlets here, thou honor- 90
able man; prove it.

Escal. [*To Angelo*] Do you hear how he misplaces?

Pom. Sir, she came in great with child, and longing,
saving your Honor's reverence, for stewed prunes.
Sir, we had but two in the house, which at that very 95
distant time stood, as it were, in a fruit dish, a dish of
some threepence. Your Honors have seen such dishes:
they are not China dishes, but very good dishes—

Escal. Go to, go to; no matter for the dish, sir.

Pom. No, indeed, sir, not of a pin. You are therein 100
in the right—but to the point. As I say, this Mistress
Elbow, being, as I say, with child, and being great-

114. **wot:** know.
120. **Come me:** come for me.
126. **Hallowmas:** All Saints' Day, November 1.

bellied, and longing, as I said, for prunes, and having
but two in the dish, as I said, Master Froth here, this
very man, having eaten the rest, as I said, and, as I 105
say, paying for them very honestly—for, as you know,
Master Froth, I could not give you threepence again.

Froth. No, indeed.

Pom. Very well; you being then, if you be remembered, cracking the stones of the foresaid prunes— 110

Froth. Ay, so I did indeed.

Pom. Why, very well; I telling you then, if you be
remembered, that such a one and such a one were
past cure of the thing you wot of, unless they kept
very good diet, as I told you— 115

Froth. All this is true.

Pom. Why, very well, then—

Escal. Come, you are a tedious fool: to the purpose.
What was done to Elbow's wife, that he hath cause
to complain of? Come me to what was done to her. 120

Pom. Sir, your Honor cannot come to that yet.

Escal. No, sir, nor I mean it not.

Pom. Sir, but you shall come to it, by your Honor's
leave. And, I beseech you, look into Master Froth
here, sir; a man of fourscore pound a year; whose 125
father died at Hallowmas—was't not at Hallowmas,
Master Froth?—

Froth. Allhallond Eve.

Pom. Why, very well: I hope here be truths. He,
sir, sitting, as I say, in a lower chair, sir—'twas in the 130
Bunch of Grapes, where, indeed, you have a delight
to sit, have you not?

133. **open room:** public room.
158. **supposed:** deposed; sworn.

Froth. I have so; because it is an open room and good for winter.

Pom. Why, very well, then; I hope here be truths. 135

Ang. This will last out a night in Russia
When nights are longest there: I'll take my leave
And leave you to the hearing of the cause,
Hoping you'll find good cause to whip them all.

Escal. I think no less. Good morrow to your Lord- 140
     ship.   [*Exit Angelo.*]
Now, sir, come on: what was done to Elbow's wife,
     once more?

Pom. Once sir? There was nothing done to her
once.   145

Elb. I beseech you, sir, ask him what this man did
to my wife.

Pom. I beseech your Honor, ask me.

Escal. Well, sir, what did this gentleman to her?

Pom. I beseech you, sir, look in this gentleman's 150
face. Good Master Froth, look upon His Honor; 'tis
for a good purpose. Doth your Honor mark his face?

Escal. Ay, sir, very well.

Pom. Nay, I beseech you, mark it well.

Escal. Well, I do so.   155

Pom. Doth your Honor see any harm in his face?

Escal. Why, no.

Pom. I'll be supposed upon a book, his face is the
worst thing about him. Good, then; if his face be the
worst thing about him, how could Master Froth do 160
the constable's wife any harm? I would know that of
your Honor.

166. **respected:** suspected.

175. **Justice . . . Iniquity:** two characters common in morality plays, referring here to Elbow and Pompey.

177. **caitiff:** base wretch.

178. **Hannibal:** error for "cannibal."

Escal. He's in the right. Constable, what say you
to it?

Elb. First, and it like you, the house is a respected 165
house; next, this is a respected fellow; and his mistress is a respected woman.

Pom. By this hand, sir, his wife is a more respected
person than any of us all.

Elb. Varlet, thou liest! Thou liest, wicked varlet! 170
The time is yet to come that she was ever respected
with man, woman, or child.

Pom. Sir, she was respected with him before he
married with her.

Escal. Which is the wiser here? Justice or Iniquity? 175
Is this true?

Elb. O thou caitiff! O thou varlet! O thou wicked
Hannibal! I respected with her before I was married
to her! If ever I was respected with her, or she with
me, let not your Worship think me the poor Duke's 180
officer. Prove this, thou wicked Hannibal, or I'll have
mine action of batt'ry on thee.

Escal. If he took you a box o' the ear, you might
have your action of slander too.

Elb. Marry, I thank your good Worship for it. 185
What is't your Worship's pleasure I shall do with this
wicked caitiff?

Escal. Truly, officer, because he hath some offenses
in him that thou wouldst discover if thou couldst, let
him continue in his courses till thou knowst what 190
they are.

Elb. Marry, I thank your Worship for it. Thou

208–9. they will draw you . . . and you will hang them: a reference to the hanging, drawing, and quartering of traitors, with a pun on Froth's name and the head of foam on ale drawn from a tap.

220. bum: slang for "bottom."

seest, thou wicked varlet, now, what's come ~
thee. Thou art to continue now, thou varlet; thou a.
to continue.

Escal. [*To Froth*] Where were you born, friend?

Froth. Here in Vienna, sir.

Escal. Are you of fourscore pounds a year?

Froth. Yes, and't please you, sir.

Escal. So. [*To Pompey*] What trade are you of, sir?   200

Pom. A tapster, a poor widow's tapster.

Escal. Your mistress' name?

Pom. Mistress Overdone.

Escal. Hath she had any more than one husband?

Pom. Nine, sir; Overdone by the last.   205

Escal. Nine! Come hither to me, Master Froth.
Master Froth, I would not have you acquainted with
tapsters: they will draw you, Master Froth, and you
will hang them. Get you gone, and let me hear no
more of you.   210

Froth. I thank your Worship. For mine own part, I
never come into any room in a taphouse but I am
drawn in.

Escal. Well, no more of it, Master Froth: farewell.
[*Exit Froth.*] Come you hither to me, Master Tapster.   215
What's your name, Master Tapster?

Pom. Pompey.

Escal. What else?

Pom. Bum, sir.

Escal. Troth, and your bum is the greatest thing   220
about you, so that, in the beastliest sense, you are
Pompey the Great. Pompey, you are partly a bawd,

223. **color:** disguise.

237. **drabs:** harlots.

244. **after:** at the rate of.

245. **bay:** that part of a house lying under one gable.

252. **shrewd:** painful. An allusion to the wars between Julius Caesar and Pompey the Great, in which Pompey was defeated.

Pompey, howsoever you color it in being a tapster,
are you not? Come, tell me true: it shall be the better
for you.   225

Pom. Truly, sir, I am a poor fellow that would live.

Escal. How would you live, Pompey? By being a
bawd? What do you think of the trade, Pompey? Is
it a lawful trade?

Pom. If the law would allow it, sir.   230

Escal. But the law will not allow it, Pompey; nor it
shall not be allowed in Vienna.

Pom. Does your Worship mean to geld and splay
all the youth of the city?

Escal. No, Pompey.   235

Pom. Truly, sir, in my poor opinion, they will to't,
then. If your Worship will take order for the drabs
and the knaves, you need not to fear the bawds.

Escal. There is pretty orders beginning, I can tell
you: it is but heading and hanging.   240

Pom. If you head and hang all that offend that way
but for ten year together, you'll be glad to give out a
commission for more heads. If this law hold in Vienna
ten year, I'll rent the fairest house in it after threepence a bay. If you live to see this come to pass, say   245
Pompey told you so.

Escal. Thank you, good Pompey; and, in requital
of your prophecy, hark you: I advise you, let me not
find you before me again upon any complaint whatsoever; no, not for dwelling where you do. If I do,   250
Pompey, I shall beat you to your tent and prove a
shrewd Caesar to you. In plain dealing, Pompey, I

258. **carman:** carter; **jade:** nag.
269. **put you so oft upon't:** employ you so
steadily.
270. **sufficient:** competent.

shall have you whipt. So, for this time, Pompey, fare
you well.

Pom. I thank your Worship for your good counsel— 255
[*Aside*] but I shall follow it as the flesh and fortune
shall better determine.
Whip me? No, no; let carman whip his jade:
The valiant heart's not whipt out of his trade.   *Exit.*

Escal. Come hither to me, Master Elbow. Come 260
hither, Master Constable. How long have you been in
this place of constable?

Elb. Seven year and a half, sir.

Escal. I thought, by the readiness in the office, you
had continued in it some time. You say, seven years 265
together?

Elb. And a half, sir.

Escal. Alas, it hath been great pains to you. They
do you wrong to put you so oft upon't. Are there not
men in your ward sufficient to serve it?   270

Elb. Faith, sir, few of any wit in such matters. As
they are chosen, they are glad to choose me for them.
I do it for some piece of money and go through with
all.

Escal. Look you bring me in the names of some six 275
or seven, the most sufficient of your parish.

Elb. To your Worship's house, sir?

Escal. To my house. Fare you well. [*Exit Elbow.*]
What's o'clock, think you?

Justice. Eleven, sir.   280

Escal. I pray you home to dinner with me.

Justice. I humbly thank you.

288. **still**: always.

||||||||||||||||||||||||||||||||||||||||||||||||||

II.ii. The provost of the prison visits Angelo to make certain that Angelo's sentence on Claudio stands, which the deputy confirms. Isabella and Lucio are admitted. Although Isabella begins her appeal in a lukewarm spirit, with Lucio's encouragement she gradually gains in eloquence and appeals to Angelo in the name of mercy and common humanity. Angelo, at first unmoved, begins to soften as Isabella's beauty stirs his senses, and he promises to think it over. He tells her to return the next day. Angelo is amazed that the saintly Isabella could so stir his emotions.

||||||||||||||||||||||||||||||||||||||||

6. **sects**: classes.
13. **Under your good correction**: an apology for what he is about to say that may be offensive.

Escal. It grieves me for the death of Claudio;
But there's no remedy.

Justice. Lord Angelo is severe.   285

Escal.   It is but needful.
Mercy is not itself that oft looks so;
Pardon is still the nurse of second woe.
But yet, poor Claudio! There is no remedy.
Come, sir.   290

Exeunt.

Scene II. [Another room in Angelo's house.]

Enter Provost [and a] Servant.

Ser. He's hearing of a cause; he will come straight.
I'll tell him of you.

Pro.   Pray you, do. [*Exit Servant.*] I'll know
His pleasure: may be he will relent. Alas,
He hath but as offended in a dream!   5
All sects, all ages smack of this vice—and he
To die for't!

Enter Angelo.

Ang.   Now, what's the matter, provost?

Pro. Is it your will Claudio shall die tomorrow?

Ang. Did not I tell thee yea? Hadst thou not order?   10
Why dost thou ask again?

Pro.   Lest I might be too rash.
Under your good correction, I have seen

16. **mine:** i.e., my worry.

When, after execution, Judgment hath
Repented o'er his doom.   15

    Ang.   Go to; let that be mine.
Do you your office, or give up your place,
And you shall well be spared.

    Pro.   I crave your Honor's pardon.
What shall be done, sir, with the groaning Juliet?   20
She's very near her hour.

    Ang.   Dispose of her
To some more fitter place, and that with speed.

[Enter Servant.]

    Ser. Here is the sister of the man condemned
Desires access to you.   25

    Ang.   Hath he a sister?

    Pro. Ay, my good lord; a very virtuous maid
And to be shortly of a sisterhood,
If not already.

    Ang.   Well, let her be admitted.   30
                               [Exit Servant.]

See you the fornicatress be removed.
Let her have needful but not lavish means:
There shall be order for't.

Enter Lucio and Isabella.

    Pro.   Save your Honor!

    Ang. Stay a little while. *[To Isabella]* Y'are wel-   35
    come: what's your will?

47–48. let it be his fault/And not my brother: cf. the proverbial "Be angry with (condemn) the vice, not the man."

51. ere it be done: i.e., by the law prohibiting it.

52. cipher: nullity.

53. fine the faults whose fine stands in record: punish by moral condemnation faults already condemned as such in the statutes.

Isa. I am a woeful suitor to your Honor,
Please but your Honor hear me.

Ang.   Well, what's your suit?

Isa. There is a vice that most I do abhor   40
And most desire should meet the blow of justice;
For which I would not plead but that I must;
For which I must not plead but that I am
At war 'twixt will and will not.

Ang.   Well, the matter?   45

Isa. I have a brother is condemned to die:
I do beseech you, let it be his fault
And not my brother.

Pro. [*Aside*]   Heaven give thee moving graces!

Ang. Condemn the fault and not the actor of it?   50
Why, every fault's condemned ere it be done.
Mine were the very cipher of a function,
To fine the faults whose fine stands in record,
And let go by the actor.

Isa.   O just but severe law!   55
I had a brother, then.—Heaven keep your Honor!

Lucio. [*Aside to Isabella*] Give't not o'er so: to him
    again, entreat him;
Kneel down before him, hang upon his gown.
You are too cold; if you should need a pin,   60
You could not with more tame a tongue desire it.
To him, I say!

Isa. Must he needs die?

Ang.   Maiden, no remedy.

Isa. Yes, I do think that you might pardon him   65
And neither Heaven nor man grieve at the mercy.

69. **Look what I will not:** whatever I will not; i.e., he cannot do what his will forbids.

71. **remorse:** pity.

77. **'longs:** belongs.

79. **truncheon:** baton of office.

90–91. **there's the vein:** that's the note to strike.

Ang. I will not do't.

Isa.   But can you, if you would?

Ang. Look what I will not, that I cannot do.

Isa. But might you do't and do the world no wrong,   70
If so your heart were touched with that remorse
As mine is to him?

Ang.   He's sentenced: 'tis too late.

Lucio. [*Aside to Isabella*] You are too cold.

Isa. Too late? Why, no; I, that do speak a word,   75
May call it back again. Well, believe this:
No ceremony that to great ones 'longs,
Not the king's crown nor the deputed sword,
The marshal's truncheon nor the judge's robe,
Become them with one half so good a grace   80
As mercy does.
If he had been as you, and you as he,
You would have slipt like him; but he, like you,
Would not have been so stern.

Ang.   Pray you, be gone.   85

Isa. I would to Heaven I had your potency
And you were Isabel! Should it then be thus?
No, I would tell what 'twere to be a judge
And what a prisoner.

Lucio. [*Aside to Isabella*] Ay, touch him; there's the   90
   vein.

Ang. Your brother is a forfeit of the law,
And you but waste your words.

Isa.   Alas, alas!
Why, all the souls that were, were forfeit once;   95
And He that might the vantage best have took

109. **of season:** at the proper season; when it is mature.

122. **Either now or by remissness new conceived:** either already conceived or likely to be if laxity of the law permits.

124. **successive degrees:** succeeding offspring.

Found out the remedy. How would you be
If He, which is the top of judgment, should
But judge you as you are? O, think on that,
And mercy then will breathe within your lips 100
Like man new made.

   Ang.   Be you content, fair maid:
It is the law not I condemn your brother.
Were he my kinsman, brother, or my son,
It should be thus with him: he must die tomorrow. 105

   Isa. Tomorrow! O, that's sudden! Spare him, spare
     him!
He's not prepared for death. Even for our kitchens
We kill the fowl of season. Shall we serve Heaven
With less respect than we do minister 110
To our gross selves? Good, good my lord, bethink you:
Who is it that hath died for this offense?
There's many have committed it.

   Lucio. [*Aside to Isabella.*]   Ay, well said.

   Ang. The law hath not been dead, though it hath 115
     slept.
Those many had not dared to do that evil,
If the first that did the edict infringe
Had answered for his deed. Now 'tis awake,
Takes note of what is done, and, like a prophet, 120
Looks in a glass that shows what future evils,
Either now or by remissness new conceived,
And so in progress to be hatched and born,
Are now to have no successive degrees
But ere they live to end. 125

   Isa.   Yet show some pity.

140. **pelting:** insignificant.

148. **glassy essence:** fragile soul; the soul's proneness to error.

150. **spleens:** the spleen was considered the organ that produced laughter.

151. **mortal:** to death.

156. **We cannot weigh our brother with ourself:** men are not competent to judge other men.

Ang. I show it most of all when I show justice;
For then I pity those I do not know,
Which a dismissed offense would after gall;
And do him right that, answering one foul wrong,   130
Lives not to act another. Be satisfied.
Your brother dies tomorrow; be content.

　Isa. So you must be the first that gives this sentence,
And he, that suffers. O, it is excellent
To have a giant's strength; but it is tyrannous   135
To use it like a giant.

　Lucio. [*Aside to Isabella*] That's well said.

　Isa. Could great men thunder
As Jove himself does, Jove would ne'er be quiet,
For every pelting, petty officer   140
Would use his heaven for thunder.
Nothing but thunder! Merciful Heaven,
Thou rather with thy sharp and sulphurous bolt
Splits the unwedgeable and gnarled oak
Than the soft myrtle; but man, proud man,   145
Drest in a little brief authority,
Most ignorant of what he's most assured,
His glassy essence, like an angry ape
Plays such fantastic tricks before high Heaven
As makes the angels weep; who, with our spleens,   150
Would all themselves laugh mortal.

　Lucio. [*Aside to Isabella*] O, to him, to him, wench!
　　He will relent.
He's coming; I perceive't.

　Pro. [*Aside*]　　　　Pray Heaven she win him! 155

　Isa. We cannot weigh our brother with ourself.

162. **avised:** advised; informed.

167. **skins the vice o' the top:** i.e., covers over its own vice. Isabella means that the authority vested in a man like Angelo has the property of making his sins inconspicuous.

174. **my sense breeds with it:** my blood is quickened by it.

184. **sickles:** a variant form of "shekels" used in the Bishop's Bible.

Great men may jest with saints; 'tis wit in them,
But in the less foul profanation.

    Lucio. Thou'rt i' the right, girl. More o' that.

    Isa. That in the captain's but a choleric word   160
Which in the soldier is flat blasphemy.

    Lucio. [*Aside to Isabella*] Art avised o' that? more
    on't.

    Ang. Why do you put these sayings upon me?

    Isa. Because authority, though it err like others,   165
Hath yet a kind of medicine in itself
That skins the vice o' the top. Go to your bosom:
Knock there and ask your heart what it doth know
That's like my brother's fault. If it confess
A natural guiltiness such as is his,   170
Let it not sound a thought upon your tongue
Against my brother's life.

    Ang. [*Aside*]   She speaks, and 'tis
Such sense that my sense breeds with it. Fare you
    well.   175

    Isa. Gentle my lord, turn back.

    Ang. I will bethink me: come again tomorrow.

    Isa. Hark how I'll bribe you: good my lord, turn
    back.

    Ang. How? bribe me?   180

    Isa. Ay, with such gifts that Heaven shall share
    with you.

    Lucio. [*Aside to Isabella*] You had marred all else.

    Isa. Not with fond sickles of the tested gold,
Or stones whose rates are either rich or poor   185
As fancy values them; but with true prayers

189. **dedicate:** dedicated.

196. **Where prayers cross:** that is, where her prayer that "His Honor" keep safe will conflict with his sinful desire to possess her.

206-7. **Do as the carrion does, not as the flow'r,/Corrupt with virtuous season:** i.e., become corrupt like a dead carcass, rather than bloom, under the beneficent rays of the sun.

209. **lightness:** wanton behavior.

That shall be up at Heaven and enter there
Ere sunrise, prayers from preserved souls,
From fasting maids whose minds are dedicate
To nothing temporal.	190
   Ang.	Well, come to me tomorrow.
   Lucio. [*Aside to Isabella*] Go to; 'tis well. Away!
   Isa. Heaven keep your Honor safe!
   Ang. [*Aside*]	Amen; for I
Am that way going to temptation,	195
Where prayers cross.
   Isa.	At what hour tomorrow
Shall I attend your Lordship?
   Ang.	At any time 'fore noon.
   Isa. Save your Honor!	200
        [*Exeunt Isabella, Lucio, and Provost.*]
   Ang.	From thee—even from thy virtue!
What's this, what's this? Is this her fault or mine?
The tempter or the tempted, who sins most, ha?
Not she; nor doth she tempt; but it is I
That, lying by the violet in the sun,	205
Do as the carrion does, not as the flow'r,
Corrupt with virtuous season. Can it be
That modesty may more betray our sense
Than woman's lightness? Having waste ground
    enough,	210
Shall we desire to raze the sanctuary,
And pitch our evils there? O, fie, fie, fie!
What dost thou, or what art thou, Angelo?
Dost thou desire her foully for those things
That make her good? O, let her brother live:	215

II.iii. The Duke in his friar's disguise visits the prison to comfort the prisoners. The provost introduces Juliet and relates her story. She appears to be truly repentant for her sin. The Duke plans to visit Claudio in order to instruct him how to meet his death in Christian fashion.

〰〰〰〰〰〰〰〰〰〰〰

4. **visit:** call upon in order to comfort.

Thieves for their robbery have authority
When judges steal themselves. What, do I love her,
That I desire to hear her speak again
And feast upon her eyes? What is't I dream on?
O cunning enemy that to catch a saint   220
With saints dost bait thy hook! Most dangerous
Is that temptation that doth goad us on
To sin in loving virtue: never could the strumpet
With all her double vigor, art, and nature
Once stir my temper; but this virtuous maid   225
Subdues me quite. Ever till now,
When men were fond, I smiled and wondered how.
                                                 Exit.

Scene III. [A room in a prison.]

Enter Duke [disguised as Friar Lodowick], and
Provost.

Duke. Hail to you, provost! so I think you are.
Pro. I am the provost. What's your will, good friar?
Duke. Bound by my charity and my blest order,
I come to visit the afflicted spirits
Here in the prison. Do me the common right   5
To let me see them and to make me know
The nature of their crimes, that I may minister
To them accordingly.
   Pro. I would do more than that, if more were need-
      ful.   10

13. **blistered her report:** damaged her reputation.

Enter Juliet.

Look, here comes one: a gentlewoman of mine,
Who, falling in the flaws of her own youth,
Hath blistered her report. She is with child
And he that got it sentenced: a young man
More fit to do another such offense   15
Than die for this.

    Duke. When must he die?

    Pro.   As I do think, tomorrow.
[*To Juliet*] I have provided for you; stay awhile
And you shall be conducted.   20

    Duke. Repent you, fair one, of the sin you carry?

    Jul. I do, and bear the shame most patiently.

    Duke. I'll teach you how you shall arraign your
      conscience
And try your penitence if it be sound   25
Or hollowly put on.

    Jul.   I'll gladly learn.

    Duke. Love you the man that wronged you?

    Jul. Yes, as I love the woman that wronged him.

    Duke. So, then, it seems your most offenseful act   30
Was mutually committed?

    Jul.   Mutually.

    Duke. Then was your sin of heavier kind than his.

    Jul. I do confess it and repent it, father.

    Duke. 'Tis meet so, daughter; but lest you do repent   35
As that the sin hath brought you to this shame,
Which sorrow is always toward ourselves, not
    Heaven,

50. **'Tis pity of him:** it's a pity about him (Claudio).

||||||||||||||||||||||||||||||||||||||||||||||||||

II.iv. Angelo cannot forget Isabella. The knowledge that he is susceptible to temptation robs him of any power to resist. When Isabella keeps her appointment, he hints that her brother may be saved. When she fails to understand, he offers to pardon Claudio in return for her love. If she refuses, Claudio will not only die but will suffer a lingering death. Isabella realizes that no one will believe her story of Angelo's attempted blackmail; yet, unable to sacrifice her honor to save her brother, she decides to help him meet death bravely.

||||||||||||||||||||||||||||||||||||||||||||

4. **invention:** fancy.

Showing we would not spare Heaven as we love it
But as we stand in fear—   40
  Jul. I do repent me as it is an evil,
And take the shame with joy.
  Duke.   There rest.
Your partner, as I hear, must die tomorrow,
And I am going with instruction to him.   45
Grace go with you! *Benedicite!*   *Exit.*
  Jul. Must die tomorrow! O injurious love,
That respites me a life whose very comfort
Is still a dying horror!
  Pro.   'Tis pity of him.   50
                            Exeunt.

Scene IV. [A room in Angelo's house.]

Enter Angelo.

  Ang. When I would pray and think, I think and
    pray
To several subjects. Heaven hath my empty words,
Whilst my invention, hearing not my tongue,
Anchors on Isabel: Heaven in my mouth,   5
As if I did but only chew his name,
And in my heart the strong and swelling evil
Of my conception. The state whereon I studied
Is like a good thing, being often read,
Grown feared and tedious. Yea, my gravity,   10
Wherein—let no man hear me—I take pride.

12. **with boot:** profitably.

13. **Which the air beats for vain:** which vainly beats the air.

14. **case:** outer covering; **habit:** garb.

17–18. **Let's write "Good Angel" on the Devil's horn;/'Tis not the Devil's crest:** i.e., if Angelo is considered virtuous, it would be appropriate to identify the Devil as a **Good Angel.**

27. **swounds:** swoons.

30. **general subject:** common people; **well-wished:** popular.

31. **Quit their own part:** leave their places.

Could I with boot change for an idle plume,
Which the air beats for vain. O place, O form,
How often dost thou with thy case, thy habit,
Wrench awe from fools and tie the wiser souls   15
To thy false seeming! Blood, thou art blood!
Let's write "Good Angel" on the Devil's horn;
'Tis not the Devil's crest.

Enter a Servant.

                    How now! who's there?
  Ser. One Isabel, a sister, desires access to you.   20
  Ang. Teach her the way. [*Exit Servant.*] O
        Heavens!
Why does my blood thus muster to my heart,
Making both it unable for itself
And dispossessing all my other parts   25
Of necessary fitness?
So play the foolish throngs with one that swounds;
Come all to help him and so stop the air
By which he should revive; and even so
The general subject to a well-wished king   30
Quit their own part and in obsequious fondness
Crowd to his presence, where their untaught love
Must needs appear offense.

Enter Isabella.

                    How now, fair maid?
  Isa. I am come to know your pleasure.   35

48–49. **from nature stol'n/A man already made:** i.e., killed a man.

50. **saucy sweetness:** lustful pleasure.

50–51. **coin Heaven's image/In stamps that are forbid:** i.e., beget children illicitly; the imagery is from counterfeiting coins.

53. **restrained:** forbidden; **means:** molds.

63–64. **Our compelled sins/Stand more for number than for accompt:** i.e., compelled sins are recorded but not counted against us.

Ang. That you might know it would much better
   please me
Than to demand what 'tis. Your brother cannot live.
  Isa. Even so.—Heaven keep your Honor!
  Ang. Yet may he live awhile, and, it may be,   40
As long as you or I. Yet he must die.
  Isa. Under your sentence?   WAGES OF
                       SIN
  Ang. Yea.
  Isa. When, I beseech you? that in his reprieve,
Longer or shorter, he may be so fitted   45
That his soul sicken not.
  Ang. Ha! fie, these filthy vices! It were as good
To pardon him that hath from nature stol'n
A man already made as to remit
Their saucy sweetness that do coin Heaven's image 50
In stamps that are forbid. 'Tis all as easy
Falsely to take away a life true made
As to put metal in restrained means
To make a false one.
  Isa. 'Tis set down so in Heaven, but not in earth. 55
  Ang. Say you so? Then I shall pose you quickly.
Which had you rather, that the most just law
Now took your brother's life, or, to redeem him,
Give up your body to such sweet uncleanness
As she that he hath stained?   60
  Isa.   Sir, believe this,
I had rather give my body than my soul.
  Ang. I talk not of your soul. Our compelled sins
Stand more for number than for accompt.
  Isa.   How say you? 65

66. **warrant:** guarantee.

72. **Pleased you to do't:** if you were pleased to do it.

76 **Were equal poise of sin and charity:** sin and charity would be balanced just as evenly.

86. **graciously:** virtuously.

88. **tax:** criticize.

89. **enshelled:** concealed, as in a shell.

91. **gross:** clearly.

Ang. Nay, I'll not warrant that; for I can speak
Against the thing I say. Answer to this:
I, now the voice of the recorded law,
Pronounce a sentence on your brother's life.
Might there not be a charity in sin   70
To save this brother's life?

Isa.   Please you to do't,
I'll take it as a peril to my soul
It is no sin at all, but charity.

Ang. Pleased you to do't at peril of your soul   75
Were equal poise of sin and charity.

Isa. That I do beg his life, if it be sin,
Heaven let me bear it! You granting of my suit,
If that be sin, I'll make it my morn prayer
To have it added to the faults of mine   80
And nothing of your answer.

Ang.   Nay, but hear me.
Your sense pursues not mine; either you are ignorant,
Or seem so, craftily, and that's not good.

Isa. Let me be ignorant and in nothing good   85
But graciously to know I am no better.

Ang. Thus wisdom wishes to appear most bright
When it doth tax itself; as these black masks
Proclaim an enshelled beauty ten times louder
Than beauty could, displayed. But mark me.   90
To be received plain, I'll speak more gross:
Your brother is to die.

Isa. So.

Ang. And his offense is so, as it appears,
Accountant to the law upon that pain.   95

98. **subscribe:** concede.

99. **But in the loss of question:** except for the sake of argument.

121. **Ignomy:** ignominy; baseness.

122. **of two houses:** unrelated.

Isa. True.

Ang. Admit no other way to save his life—
As I subscribe not that, nor any other,
But in the loss of question—that you, his sister,
Finding yourself desired of such a person   100
Whose credit with the judge, or own great place,
Could fetch your brother from the manacles
Of the all-binding law; and that there were
No earthly mean to save him but that either
You must lay down the treasures of your body   105
To this supposed, or else to let him suffer;
What would you do?

Isa. As much for my poor brother as myself:
That is, were I under the terms of death,
The impression of keen whips I'ld wear as rubies   110
And strip myself to death. as to a bed
That, longing, have been sick for, ere I'ld yield
My body up to shame.

Ang.   Then must your brother die.

Isa. And 'twere the cheaper way: 115
Better it were a brother died at once
Than that a sister, by redeeming him,
Should die forever.

Ang. Were not you, then, as cruel as the sentence
That you have slandered so?   120

Isa. Ignomy in ransom and free pardon
Are of two houses· lawful mercy
Is nothing kin to foul redemption.

Ang. You seemed of late to make the law a tyrant,

126. **merriment:** prank.

134–35. **If not a fedary but only he/Owe and succeed thy weakness:** if no accomplice shares the sin for which you have condemned him; **Owe and succeed:** own by inheritance.

137. **glasses:** a proverb had it: "Glasses and lasses are brittle ware."

138. **forms:** images.

139–40. **men their creation mar/In profiting by them:** men sully themselves when they take advantage of women's weakness.

142. **credulous to false prints:** impressionable.

143. **think it well:** fully believe it.

147. **arrest:** seize upon (as warranty for what follows).

148. **none:** i.e., not human.

151. **destined livery:** habit (conduct) destined for you as a woman.

152. **tongue:** language.

153. **former:** i.e., clear and unmistakable.

And rather proved the sliding of your brother   125
A merriment than a vice.

   Isa. O, pardon me, my lord. It oft falls out,
To have what we would have, we speak not what we
     mean.
I something do excuse the thing I hate,   130
For his advantage that I dearly love.

   Ang. We are all frail.

   Isa.   Else let my brother die,
If not a fedary but only he
Owe and succeed thy weakness.   135

   Ang. Nay, women are frail too.

   Isa. Ay, as the glasses where they view themselves,
Which are as easy broke as they make forms.
Women!—Help Heaven! men their creation mar
In profiting by them. Nay, call us ten times frail;   140
For we are soft as our complexions are
And credulous to false prints.

   Ang.   I think it well:
And from this testimony of your own sex—
Since I suppose we are made to be no stronger   145
Than faults may shake our frames—let me be bold:
I do arrest your words. Be that you are,
That is, a woman. If you be more, you're none.
If you be one—as you are well expressed
By all external warrants—show it now   150
By putting on the destined livery.

   Isa. I have no tongue but one; gentle my lord,
Let me entreat you speak the former language.

   Ang. Plainly conceive I love you.

160. **pluck on:** incite.

171. **vouch:** testimony.

175. **race:** strain.

177. **prolixious:** overextended; exaggerated.

178. **banish what they sue for:** i.e., instead of shaming him as evidences of her innocent purity, her blushes only inflame him further.

182. **sufferance:** suffering.

183. **affection:** passion.

Isa. My brother did love Juliet,   155
And you tell me that he shall die for it.

    Ang. He shall not, Isabel, if you give me love.

    Isa. I know your virtue hath a license in't,
Which seems a little fouler than it is,
To pluck on others.   160

    Ang.   Believe me, on mine honor,
My words express my purpose.

    Isa. Ha! little honor to be much believed,
And most pernicious purpose!—Seeming, seeming!—
I will proclaim thee, Angelo: look for't.   165
Sign me a present pardon for my brother,
Or with an outstretched throat I'll tell the world aloud
What man thou art.

    Ang.   Who will believe thee, Isabel?
My unsoiled name, the austereness of my life,   170
My vouch against you, and my place i' the state
Will so your accusation overweigh
That you shall stifle in your own report
And smell of calumny. I have begun;
And now I give my sensual race the rein.   175
Fit thy consent to my sharp appetite;
Lay by all nicety and prolixious blushes
That banish what they sue for. Redeem thy brother
By yielding up thy body to my will,
Or else he must not only die the death,   180
But thy unkindness shall his death draw out
To ling'ring sufferance. Answer me tomorrow,
Or by the affection that now guides me most

185. **my false o'erweighs your true:** my false denial will carry more conviction than your true accusation.

189. **approof:** approval.

194. **mind of honor:** honorable mind.

195. **tender:** offer.

I'll prove a tyrant to him. As for you,
Say what you can, my false o'erweighs your true. *Exit.* 185
  Isa. To whom should I complain? Did I tell this,
Who would believe me? O perilous mouths,
That bear in them one and the selfsame tongue,
Either of condemnation or approof;
Bidding the law make curtsy to their will;   190
Hooking both right and wrong to the appetite,
To follow as it draws! I'll to my brother.
Though he hath fall'n by prompture of the blood,
Yet hath he in him such a mind of honor
That, had he twenty heads to tender down   195
On twenty bloody blocks, he'ld yield them up
Before his sister should her body stoop
To such abhorred pollution.
Then, Isabel, live chaste, and, brother, die:
More than our brother is our chastity.   200
I'll tell him yet of Angelo's request,
And fit his mind to death, for his soul's rest.

                                     Exit.

MEASURE
FOR
MEASURE

ACT III

III.i. The Duke, finding Claudio hopeful of pardon, warns him to abandon such thoughts and accept death. Claudio appears convinced, but Isabella's arrival renews his hope. The Duke conceals himself to overhear their conversation. Isabella tells Claudio that he may be saved at the expense of her honor. Claudio at first says she must not do it, but horror at the thought of death weakens his resolution, and he begs Isabella to comply. Isabella vows that she will rather pray for his death. Before she leaves, the Duke asks her to spare him a few moments. As she awaits him, the Duke counsels Claudio that Angelo has merely made his proposal to test her and advises him again to prepare for death. The Duke then tells Isabella of Mariana, Angelo's former betrothed, whom he cast off when her dowry was lost. Since Mariana still loves Angelo, the Duke proposes that Isabella make an appointment with Angelo and arrange for Mariana to keep it. Isabella agrees and the Duke promises to inform Mariana.

‖‖‖‖‖‖‖‖‖‖‖‖‖‖‖‖‖‖‖‖‖‖‖‖‖‖‖‖‖‖‖‖

6. **absolute:** resolute; determined.

10. **skyey:** astronomical. The Elizabethans firmly believed that the heavenly bodies influenced human affairs.

11. **keepst:** dwellest.

12. **Merely thou art Death's fool:** you are nothing but Death's plaything.

15. **accommodations:** furnishings; conveniences.

16. **nursed by baseness:** cherished by your ignoble traits.

ACT III

Scene I. [A room in the prison.]

Enter Duke [disguised], Claudio, and Provost.

Duke. So, then, you hope of pardon from Lord
    Angelo?
    Claud. The miserable have no other medicine
But only hope:
I've hope to live, and am prepared to die.   5
    Duke. Be absolute for death: either death or life
Shall thereby be the sweeter. Reason thus with life:
If I do lose thee, I do lose a thing
That none but fools would keep. A breath thou art,
Servile to all the skyey influences   10
That dost this habitation where thou keepst
Hourly afflict. Merely thou art Death's fool;
For him thou laborst by thy flight to shun
And yet runnst toward him still. Thou art not noble;
For all the accommodations that thou bearst   15
Are nursed by baseness. Thou'rt by no means valiant;
For thou dost fear the soft and tender fork
Of a poor worm. Thy best of rest is sleep,
And that thou oft provokst; yet grossly fearst
Thy death, which is no more. Thou art not thyself; 20

46

24. **certain:** stable.

25–26. **thy complexion shifts to strange effects /After the moon:** your disposition is strangely altered by the moon's influence.

32. **serpigo:** ringworm, or a similar skin disease; **rheum:** catarrh

37–38. **Becomes as aged and doth beg the alms/Of palsied eld:** acts like an old man and begs alms as do other indigent old men; **palsied eld:** trembling old men.

39. **affection:** passion; **limb:** soundness of limb.

43. **makes these odds all even:** abolishes all these troubles.

For thou exists on many a thousand grains
That issue out of dust. Happy thou art not;
For what thou hast not, still thou strivest to get,
And what thou hast, forgetst. Thou art not certain;
For thy complexion shifts to strange effects   25
After the moon. If thou art rich, thou'rt poor;
For, like an ass whose back with ingots bows,
Thou bearst thy heavy riches but a journey
And death unloads thee. Friend hast thou none;
For thine own bowels, which do call thee sire,   30
The mere effusion of thy proper loins,
Do curse the gout, serpigo, and the rheum
For ending thee no sooner. Thou hast nor youth nor
        age,
But, as it were, an after-dinner's sleep,   35
Dreaming on both; for all thy blessed youth
Becomes as aged and doth beg the alms
Of palsied eld; and when thou art old and rich,
Thou hast neither heat, affection, limb, nor beauty
To make thy riches pleasant. What's yet in this   40
That bears the name of life? Yet in this life
Lie hid mo thousand deaths; yet death we fear,
That makes these odds all even.
    Claud.   I humbly thank you.
To sue to live, I find I seek to die;   45
And, seeking death, find life: let it come on.
    Isa. [*Within*] What, ho! Peace here, grace and good
        company!
    Pro. Who's there? Come in: the wish deserves a
welcome.   50

65. **leiger:** resident ambassador.

66. **appointment:** preparation.

76. **durance:** imprisonment

77–79. **a restraint,/Though all the world's vastidity you had,/To a determined scope:** confinement, although you were free to range through the vast world, to the single thought of your own baseness.

Duke. Dear sir, ere long I'll visit you again.
Claud. Most holy sir, I thank you.

Enter Isabella.

Isa. My business is a word or two with Claudio.
Pro. And very welcome. Look, signior, here's your
    sister.   55
Duke. Provost, a word with you.
Pro. As many as you please.
Duke. Bring me to hear them speak, where I may
    be concealed.   [*Exeunt Duke and Provost.*]
Claud. Now, sister, what's the comfort?   60
Isa. Why,
As all comforts are; most good, most good indeed.
Lord Angelo, having affairs to Heaven,
Intends you for his swift ambassador,
Where you shall be an everlasting leiger.   65
Therefore your best appointment make with speed;
Tomorrow you set on.
Claud.   Is there no remedy?
Isa. None but such remedy as, to save a head,
To cleave a heart in twain.   70
Claud.   But is there any?
Isa. Yes, brother, you may live.
There is a devilish mercy in the judge,
If you'll implore it, that will free your life
But fetter you till death.   75
Claud.   Perpetual durance?
Isa. Ay, just; perpetual durance, a restraint,

86. **feverous:** feverish; sickly; **entertain:** maintain; welcome.

94. **resolution:** courage.

102. **appliances:** expedients.

103. **settled:** set; stern.

104. **Nips youth i' the head:** nips youthful folly in the bud; **enew:** drive into water, as a falcon does his prey. There may be a thought of the ducking of witches and scolds, since the sense requires that the treatment have a chastening effect.

106. **cast:** ejected.

Though all the world's vastidity you had,
To a determined scope.

    Claud.   But in what nature?   80

    Isa. In such a one as, you consenting to't,
Would bark your honor from that trunk you bear
And leave you naked.

    Claud.   Let me know the point.

    Isa. O, I do fear thee, Claudio; and I quake,   85
Lest thou a feverous life shouldst entertain
And six or seven winters more respect
Than a perpetual honor. Darest thou die?
The sense of death is most in apprehension;
And the poor beetle that we tread upon   90
In corporal sufferance finds a pang as great
As when a giant dies.

    Claud.   Why give you me this shame?
Think you I can a resolution fetch
From flow'ry tenderness? If I must die,   95
I will encounter darkness as a bride
And hug it in mine arms.

    Isa. There spake my brother; there my father's
        grave
Did utter forth a voice. Yes, thou must die: 100
Thou art too noble to conserve a life
In base appliances. This outward-sainted deputy,
Whose settled visage and deliberate word
Nips youth i' the head and follies doth enew
As falcon doth the fowl, is yet a devil;   105
His filth within being cast, he would appear
A pond as deep as hell.

108. **prenzie:** this word has defied annotators and lexicographers. It may be a misprint for "precise," meaning "puritanical."

111. **guards:** decorative trimmings, such as braid.

123. **frankly:** generously.

128. **force:** enforce.

132. **trick:** frolic.

133. **perdurably fined:** eternally punished.

Claud. The prenzie, Angelo!

Isa. O, 'tis the cunning livery of hell,
The damned'st body to invest and cover 110
In prenzie guards! Dost thou think, Claudio?—
If I would yield him my virginity,
Thou mightst be freed!

Claud. O Heavens! it cannot be.

Isa. Yes, he would give't thee, from this rank 115
    offense,
So to offend him still. This night's the time
That I should do what I abhor to name,
Or else thou diest tomorrow.

Claud. Thou shalt not do't. 120

Isa. O, were it but my life,
I'd throw it down for your deliverance
As frankly as a pin.

Claud. Thanks, dear Isabel.

Isa. Be ready, Claudio, for your death tomorrow. 125

Claud. Yes. Has he affections in him,
That thus can make him bite the law by the nose,
When he would force it? Sure, it is no sin;
Or of the deadly seven it is the least.

Isa. Which is the least? 130

Claud. If it were damnable, he being so wise,
Why would he for the momentary trick
Be perdurably fined?—O Isabel!

Isa. What says my brother?

Claud. Death is a fearful thing. 135

Isa. And shamed life a hateful.

Claud. Ay, but to die and go we know not where;

138. **in cold obstruction:** i.e., imprisoned in the cold earth.

139. **sensible:** sensitive.

140. **kneaded clod:** worked-over lump of earth; **delighted:** capable of delight.

142. **thrilling:** piercing.

143. **viewless:** unseen; invisible.

155. **dispenses with:** offers dispensation for; forgives.

162. **shield:** forbid.

163. **warped slip of wilderness:** crooked scion (offspring).

To lie in cold obstruction and to rot;
This sensible warm motion to become
A kneaded clod; and the delighted spirit 140
To bathe in fiery floods, or to reside
In thrilling region of thick-ribbed ice;
To be imprisoned in the viewless winds
And blown with restless violence round about
The pendent world; or to be worse than worst 145
Of those that lawless and incertain thought
Imagine howling! 'Tis too horrible!
The weariest and most loathed worldly life
That age, ache, penury, and imprisonment
Can lay on nature is a paradise 150
To what we fear of death.
   Isa. Alas, alas!
   Claud.   Sweet sister, let me live:
What sin you do to save a brother's life,
Nature dispenses with the deed so far 155
That it becomes a virtue.
   Isa.   O you beast!
O faithless coward! O dishonest wretch!
Wilt thou be made a man out of my vice?
Is't not a kind of incest to take life 160
From thine own sister's shame? What should I think?
Heaven shield my mother played my father fair!
For such a warped slip of wilderness
Ne'er issued from his blood. Take my defiance!
Die, perish! Might but my bending down 165
Reprieve thee from thy fate, it should proceed.

179. **by and by:** immediately.

188–89. **disposition of natures:** classification of characters.

190. **gracious:** virtuous.

193–94. **satisfy your resolution with hopes that are fallible:** comfort yourself with false hopes.

I'll pray a thousand prayers for thy death,
No word to save thee.

   Claud. Nay, hear me, Isabel.

   Isa.   O fie, fie, fie!   170
Thy sin's not accidental but a trade.
Mercy to thee would prove itself a bawd:
'Tis best that thou diest quickly.

   Claud.   \   O, hear me, Isabella!

[Enter Duke.]

   Duke. Vouchsafe a word, young sister, but one 175
    word.

   Isa. What is your will?

   Duke. Might you dispense with your leisure, I
would by and by have some speech with you. The
satisfaction I would require is likewise your own 180
benefit.

   Isa. I have no superfluous leisure: my stay must be
stolen out of other affairs; but I will attend you
awhile.   *[Walks apart.]*

   Duke. Son, I have overheard what hath passed be- 185
tween you and your sister. Angelo had never the purpose to corrupt her; only he hath made an assay of
her virtue to practice his judgment with the disposition of natures. She, having the truth of honor in her,
hath made him that gracious denial which he is most 190
glad to receive. I am confessor to Angelo, and I know
this to be true. Therefore prepare yourself to death.
Do not satisfy your resolution with hopes that are

198. **Hold you there:** keep to that plan.

203. **loss:** injury.

205. **In good time:** very well.

207–8. **The goodness that is cheap in beauty makes beauty brief in goodness:** i.e., "Beauty and honesty seldom agree," as the proverb said.

209. **complexion:** nature (not facial appearance).

215. **resolve:** answer definitely.

fallible: tomorrow you must die. Go to your knees
and make ready.   195

Claud. Let me ask my sister pardon. I am so out of
love with life that I will sue to be rid of it.

Duke. Hold you there: farewell. [*Exit Claudio.*]
Provost, a word with you!

[*Enter Provost.*]

Pro. What's your will, father?   200

Duke. That now you are come, you will be gone.
Leave me awhile with the maid. My mind promises
with my habit no loss shall touch her by my company.

Pro. In good time.   *Exit.* 205

[*Isabella comes forward.*]

Duke. The hand that hath made you fair hath made
you good. The goodness that is cheap in beauty
makes beauty brief in goodness; but grace, being the
soul of your complexion, shall keep the body of it
ever fair. The assault that Angelo hath made to you 210
fortune hath conveyed to my understanding; and, but
that frailty hath examples for his falling, I should
wonder at Angelo. How will you do to content this
substitute and to save your brother?

Isa. I am now going to resolve him. I had rather 215
my brother die by the law than my son should be
unlawfully born. But, O, how much is the good Duke

219–20. discover his government: reveal how he conducts himself.

222. avoid: refute.

241. limit: limiting date.

242. solemnity: performance of the marriage rites.

247. sinew: pith; strength.

deceived in Angelo! If ever he return and I can speak
to him, I will open my lips in vain or discover his
government.   220

Duke. That shall not be much amiss. Yet, as the
matter now stands, he will avoid your accusation: he
made trial of you only. Therefore fasten your ear on
my advisings. To the love I have in doing good a
remedy presents itself. I do make myself believe that 225
you may most uprighteously do a poor wronged lady
a merited benefit, redeem your brother from the angry law, do no stain to your own gracious person,
and much please the absent Duke, if peradventure
he shall ever return to have hearing of this business. 230

Isa. Let me hear you speak farther. I have spirit to
do anything that appears not foul in the truth of my
spirit.

Duke. Virtue is bold and goodness never fearful.
Have you not heard speak of Mariana, the sister of 235
Frederick, the great soldier who miscarried at sea?

Isa. I have heard of the lady, and good words went
with her name.

Duke. She should this Angelo have married; was
affianced to her by oath, and the nuptial appointed: 240
between which time of the contract and limit of the
solemnity her brother Frederick was wracked at sea,
having in that perished vessel the dowry of his sister.
But mark how heavily this befell to the poor gentlewoman: there she lost a noble and renowned brother, 245
in his love toward her ever most kind and natural;
with him, the portion and sinew of her fortune, her

248. **combinate:** betrothed.
271. **refer yourself:** have recourse.
276. **stead up:** fulfill.

marriage dowry, with both, her combinate husband,
this well-seeming Angelo.

Isa. Can this be so? Did Angelo so leave her?   250

Duke. Left her in her tears and dried not one of
them with his comfort; swallowed his vows whole,
pretending in her discoveries of dishonor: in few,
bestowed her on her own lamentation, which she yet
wears for his sake; and he, a marble to her tears, is 255
washed with them, but relents not.

Isa. What a merit were it in death to take this poor
maid from the world! What corruption in this life
that it will let this man live! But how out of this can
she avail?   260

Duke. It is a rupture that you may easily heal; and
the cure of it not only saves your brother but keeps
you from dishonor in doing it.

Isa. Show me how, good father.

Duke. This forenamed maid hath yet in her the 265
continuance of her first affection. His unjust unkindness, that in all reason should have quenched her
love, hath, like an impediment in the current, made
it more violent and unruly. Go you to Angelo; answer his requiring with a plausible obedience; agree 270
with his demands to the point; only refer yourself to
this advantage, first, that your stay with him may not
be long; that the time may have all shadow and silence in it and the place answer to convenience. This
being granted in course—and now follows all—we 275
shall advise this wronged maid to stead up your appointment, go in your place. If the encounter ac-

281. **scaled:** captured (as by scaling a wall); **frame:** prepare.

287. **holding up:** carrying it through.

290. **grange:** country house.

291. **dejected:** rejected.

292. **dispatch:** arrange.

⸻

III.[ii.] Outside the prison the Duke observes Elbow with Pompey in custody. Lucio appears and taunts Pompey, then engages the Duke in conversation. Lucio freely criticizes the cold nature of Angelo and charges that Duke Vincentio is more susceptible to sins of the flesh. The Duke is indignant and warns Lucio that he may have to pay for his words when the Duke returns. Escalus and the provost then bring along Mistress Overdone, who has been arrested on Lucio's information, as she complains, asserting that she has kept Lucio's child by another woman ever since it was born. Escalus orders officers to arrest the licentious Lucio. Since Claudio is condemned to die the following day, Escalus commands that he be given spiritual consolation. The provost indicates that the Duke has already visited him, and the latter reports that Claudio is reconciled to his death. Escalus regrets the severity of Angelo's justice. The Duke remarks that if Angelo conducts his own life in keeping with his strict justice, he does well; if not, he has passed his own sentence.

⸻

4. **bastard:** a sweet Spanish wine, with a pun.

knowledge itself hereafter, it may compel him to her
recompense; and here, by this, is your brother saved,
your honor untainted, the poor Mariana advantaged, 280
and the corrupt deputy scaled. The maid will I frame
and make fit for his attempt. If you think well to carry
this as you may, the doubleness of the benefit de-
fends the deceit from reproof. What think you of it?

Isa. The image of it gives me content already; and 285
I trust it will grow to a most prosperous perfection.

Duke. It lies much in your holding up. Haste you
speedily to Angelo. If for this night he entreat you
to his bed, give him promise of satisfaction. I will
presently to St. Luke's: there, at the moated grange, 290
resides this dejected Mariana. At that place call upon
me; and dispatch with Angelo that it may be quickly.

Isa. I thank you for this comfort. Fare you well,
good father.

Exeunt.

[Scene II. The street before the prison.]

*Enter, [on one side, Duke disguised; on the other,]
Elbow, Clown, [and] Officers.*

Elb. Nay, if there be no remedy for it, but that you
will needs buy and sell men and women like beasts,
we shall have all the world drink brown and white
bastard.

Duke. O Heavens! what stuff is here? 5

8. **furred gown:** usurers commonly wore gowns trimmed with fox and lambskin. **By order of law** refers to the statutes regulating dress according to class.

10. **craft:** i.e., symbolized by the fox fur; **innocency:** the lambskin with which the gown was faced on the inside.

A usurer in his furred gown. From John Blaxton, *The English Usurer* (1623).

Pom. 'Twas never merry world since, of two usu-
ries, the merriest was put down and the worser allowed by order of law a furred gown to keep him
warm; and furred with fox and lambskins too, to sig-
nify that craft, being richer than innocency, stands   10
for the facing.

Elb. Come your way, sir. Bless you, good father
friar.

Duke. And you, good brother father. What offense
hath this man made you, sir?   15

Elb. Marry, sir, he hath offended the law: and, sir,
we take him to be a thief too, sir; for we have found
upon him, sir, a strange picklock, which we have sent
to the deputy.

Duke. Fie, sirrah! a bawd, a wicked bawd!   20
The evil that thou causest to be done,
That is thy means to live. Do thou but think
What 'tis to cram a maw or clothe a back
From such a filthy vice. Say to thyself,
From their abominable and beastly touches   25
I drink, I eat, array myself, and live.
Canst thou believe thy living is a life,
So stinkingly depending? Go mend, go mend.

Pom. Indeed, it does stink in some sort, sir; but
yet, sir, I would prove—   30

Duke. Nay, if the Devil hath given thee proofs for
sin,
Thou wilt prove his. Take him to prison, officer.
Correction and instruction must both work
Ere this rude beast will profit.   35

39. **go a mile on his errand:** i.e., he will already be far gone.

41. **Free from our faults, as faults from seeming free:** i.e., as free of faults as our faults are obvious.

42. **His neck will come to your waist:** i.e., he will be hanged with a cord like that of the friar's girdle.

48–49. **putting the hand in the pocket and extracting it clutched:** making money from prostitutes.

51. **drowned i' the last rain:** possibly a pun on "rain/reign," referring to the new enforcement of laws under Angelo's government; **trot:** old woman.

53. **sad:** serious; **The trick of it:** how goes it? What's the way of it?

58. **In the tub:** being treated in a tub for venereal disease.

60. **powdered:** salted. The treatment vats for venereal disease were called "powdering tubs."

61. **unshunned:** unavoidable; i.e., the one condition invariably leads to the other.

Elb. He must before the deputy, sir; he has given
him warning. The deputy cannot abide a whoremas-
ter. If he be a whoremonger and comes before him,
he were as good go a mile on his errand.

Duke. That we were all, as some would seem to be,   40
Free from our faults, as faults from seeming free!

Elb. His neck will come to your waist—a cord, sir.

Pom. I spy comfort. I cry bail. Here's a gentleman
and a friend of mine.

Enter Lucio.

Lucio. How now, noble Pompey! What, at the   45
wheels of Caesar? Art thou led in triumph? What, is
there none of Pygmalion's images, newly made woman, to be had now, for putting the hand in the pocket
and extracting it clutched? What reply, ha? What
sayst thou to this tune, matter, and method? Is't not   50
drowned i' the last rain, ha? What sayst thou, trot?
Is the world as it was, man? Which is the way? Is it
sad and few words? or how? The trick of it?

Duke. [*Aside*] Still thus and thus; still worse!

Lucio. How doth my dear morsel, thy mistress?   55
Procures she still, ha?

Pom. Troth, sir, she hath eaten up all her beef, and
she is herself in the tub.

Lucio. Why, 'tis good. It is the right of it. It must
be so. Ever your fresh whore and your powdered   60
bawd: an unshunned consequence. It must be so.
Art going to prison, Pompey?

76. **wear:** fashion; thing to do.
77. **mettle:** (1) spirit; (2) metal (of his fetters).

A fettered prisoner before the judges. From Joost Damhouder,
Praxis rerum criminalium (1562).

Pom. Yes, faith, sir.

Lucio. Why, 'tis not amiss, Pompey. Farewell: go say I sent thee thither. For debt, Pompey? or how?   65

Elb. For being a bawd, for being a bawd.

Lucio. Well, then, imprison him. If imprisonment be the due of a bawd, why, 'tis his right. Bawd is he doubtless, and of antiquity too: bawd-born. Farewell, good Pompey. Commend me to the prison,   70 Pompey. You will turn good husband now, Pompey; you will keep the house.

Pom. I hope, sir, your good Worship will be my bail.

Lucio. No, indeed, will I not, Pompey: it is not the   75 wear. I will pray, Pompey, to increase your bondage. If you take it not patiently, why, your mettle is the more. Adieu, trusty Pompey. Bless you, friar.

Duke. And you.

Lucio. Does Bridget paint still, Pompey, ha?   80

Elb. Come your ways, sir, come.

Pom. You will not bail me, then, sir?

Lucio. Then, Pompey, nor now. What news abroad, friar? what news?

Elb. Come your ways, sir, come.   85

Lucio. Go to kennel, Pompey; go.

             [*Exeunt Elbow, Pompey and Officers.*]

What news, friar, of the Duke?

Duke. I know none. Can you tell me of any?

Lucio. Some say he is with the Emperor of Russia; othersome, he is in Rome. But where is he, think   90 you?

97. **puts transgression to't:** gives wrongdoers a bad time.

103. **sooth:** truth.

104. **extirp:** destroy.

111. **stockfishes:** dried, salted cod.

113–14. **motion generative:** i.e., no more capable of generation than a puppet. **Motion** is the usual Elizabethan word for "puppet."

115. **pleasant:** facetious; **apace:** quickly and thoughtlessly.

Duke. I know not where; but wheresoever, I wish him well.

Lucio. It was a mad fantastical trick of him to steal from the state and usurp the beggary he was never 95 born to. Lord Angelo dukes it well in his absence: he puts transgression to't.

Duke. He does well in't.

Lucio. A little more lenity to lechery would do no harm in him: something too crabbed that way, friar. 100

Duke. It is too general a vice, and severity must cure it.

Lucio. Yes, in good sooth, the vice is of a great kindred; it is well allied; but it is impossible to extirp it quite, friar, till eating and drinking be put down. 105 They say this Angelo was not made by man and woman after the downright way of creation. Is it true, think you?

Duke. How should he be made, then?

Lucio. Some report a sea-maid spawned him; some, 110 that he was begot between two stockfishes. But it is certain that when he makes water his urine is congealed ice: that I know to be true. And he is a motion generative: that's infallible.

Duke. You are pleasant, sir, and speak apace. 115

Lucio. Why, what a ruthless thing is this in him, for the rebellion of a codpiece to take away the life of a man! Would the Duke that is absent have done this? Ere he would have hanged a man for the getting a hundred bastards, he would have paid for the 120 nursing a thousand. He had some feeling of the

124–25. **detected:** accused.

129. **use:** custom.

129–30. **clack-dish:** wooden dish with a cover that was clattered to attract attention.

133. **inward:** intimate.

139. **the greater file of the subject:** most of the rank and file of the people.

142. **unweighing:** thoughtless.

146. **helmed:** steered.

146–47. **give him a better proclamation:** proclaim him better (than Lucio describes him).

148. **bringings-forth:** deeds.

150. **unskillfully:** ignorantly.

sport; he knew the service, and that instructed him to mercy.

Duke. I never heard the absent Duke much de- tected for women. He was not inclined that way. 125

Lucio. O, sir, you are deceived.

Duke. 'Tis not possible.

Lucio. Who, not the Duke? Yes, your beggar of fifty; and his use was to put a ducat in her clack- dish. The Duke had crotchets in him. He would be 130 drunk too; that let me inform you.

Duke. You do him wrong, surely.

Lucio. Sir, I was an inward of his. A shy fellow was the Duke; and I believe I know the cause of his with- drawing. 135

Duke. What, I prithee, might be the cause?

Lucio. No, pardon; 'tis a secret must be locked within the teeth and the lips. But this I can let you understand; the greater file of the subject held the Duke to be wise. 140

Duke. Wise! why, no question but he was.

Lucio. A very superficial, ignorant, unweighing fel- low.

Duke. Either this is envy in you, folly, or mistak- ing: the very stream of his life and the business he 145 hath helmed must, upon a warranted need, give him a better proclamation. Let him be but testimonied in his own bringings-forth and he shall appear to the envious a scholar, a statesman, and a soldier. There- fore you speak unskillfully; or if your knowledge be 150 more, it is much darkened in your malice.

168. **opposite:** enemy.
175. **tundish:** funnel.
177. **ungenitured:** impotent.

Lucio. Sir, I know him, and I love him.

Duke. Love talks with better knowledge and knowledge with dearer love.

Lucio. Come, sir, I know what I know.   155

Duke. I can hardly believe that, since you know not what you speak. But if ever the Duke return, as our prayers are he may, let me desire you to make your answer before him. If it be honest you have spoke, you have courage to maintain it. I am bound 160 to call upon you; and, I pray you, your name?

Lucio. Sir, my name is Lucio; well known to the Duke.

Duke. He shall know you better, sir, if I may live to report you.   165

Lucio. I fear you not.

Duke. O, you hope the Duke will return no more; or you imagine me too unhurtful an opposite. But, indeed, I can do you little harm: you'll forswear this again.   170

Lucio. I'll be hanged first. Thou art deceived in me, friar. But no more of this. Canst thou tell if Claudio die tomorrow or no?

Duke. Why should he die, sir?

Lucio. Why? For filling a bottle with a tundish. I 175 would the Duke we talk of were returned again. This ungenitured agent will unpeople the province with continency: sparrows must not build in his house-eaves because they are lecherous. The Duke yet would have dark deeds darkly answered: he would 180 never bring them to light. Would he were returned!

182. **Marry:** verily; indeed.

184. **mutton:** slang for a loose woman; i.e., woman's flesh.

188. **mortality:** human life.

205. **Philip and Jacob:** the feast of St. Philip and St. James, May 1.

Marry, this Claudio is condemned for untrussing.
Farewell, good friar; I prithee, pray for me. The
Duke, I say to thee again, would eat mutton on Fri-
days. He's now past it; yet, and I say to thee, he 185
would mouth with a beggar, though she smelt brown
bread and garlic: say that I said so. Farewell. *Exit.*

Duke. No might nor greatness in mortality
Can censure 'scape; back-wounding calumny
The whitest virtue strikes. What king so strong 190
Can tie the gall up in the slanderous tongue?
But who comes here?

*Enter Escalus, Provost, [and Officers with Mistress
Overdone].*

Escal. Go; away with her to prison!
Mrs. Over. Good my lord, be good to me. Your
Honor is accounted a merciful man, good my lord. 195
Escal. Double and treble admonition, and still forfeit in the same kind! This would make mercy swear
and play the tyrant.
Pro. A bawd of eleven years' continuance, may it
please your Honor. 200
Mrs. Over. My lord, this is one Lucio's information against me. Mistress Kate Keepdown was with
child by him in the Duke's time. He promised her
marriage. His child is a year and a quarter old, come
Philip and Jacob. I have kept it myself; and see how 205
he goes about to abuse me!
Escal. That fellow is a fellow of much license. Let

213. **wrought:** was moved.

216. **entertainment:** welcome; reception.

220. **chance:** fortune.

222. **my time:** the time being.

231. **security:** i.e., the standing of surety for a friend. If the friend failed to meet his obligation, the surety had to pay the creditor.

232–33. **Much upon this riddle runs the wisdom of the world:** the wisdom of the world is much like this paradox.

Condemned prisoners making their last confessions. From Joost Damhouder, *Praxis rerum criminalium* (1562).

him be called before us. Away with her to prison! Go
to; no more words. [*Exeunt Officers with Mistress
Overdone.*] Provost, my brother Angelo will not be 210
altered: Claudio must die tomorrow. Let him be fur-
nished with divines and have all charitable preparation. If my brother wrought by my pity, it should not
be so with him.

Pro. So please you, this friar hath been with him 215
and advised him for the entertainment of death.

Escal. Good even, good father.

Duke. Bliss and goodness on you!

Escal. Of whence are you?

Duke. Not of this country, though my chance is 220
now
To use it for my time: I am a brother
Of gracious order, late come from the See
In special business from His Holiness.

Escal. What news abroad i' the world? 225

Duke. None but that there is so great a fever on
goodness that the dissolution of it must cure it. Nov-
elty is only in request; and it is as dangerous to be
aged in any kind of course as it is virtuous to be
constant in any undertaking. There is scarce truth 230
enough alive to make societies secure but security
enough to make fellowships accurst. Much upon this
riddle runs the wisdom of the world. This news is
old enough, yet it is every day's news. I pray you,
sir, of what disposition was the Duke? 235

Escal. One that, above all other strifes, contended
especially to know himself.

242. **events:** affairs.

245. **lent him visitation:** offered him priestly consolation.

246–47. **sinister measure:** unfair sentence.

249. **framed to himself:** imagined.

253. **paid the Heavens your function:** rendered Heaven the service appropriate to a priest.

255–56. **to the extremest shore of my modesty:** as far as I could go with propriety.

Duke. What pleasure was he given to?

Escal. Rather rejoicing to see another merry than
merry at anything which professed to make him re-   240
joice: a gentleman of all temperance. But leave we
him to his events, with a prayer they may prove prosperous; and let me desire to know how you find
Claudio prepared. I am made to understand that you
have lent him visitation.   245

Duke. He professes to have received no sinister
measure from his judge but most willingly humbles
himself to the determination of justice. Yet had he
framed to himself, by the instruction of his frailty,
many deceiving promises of life; which I, by my   250
good leisure, have discredited to him, and now is
he resolved to die.

Escal. You have paid the Heavens your function
and the prisoner the very debt of your calling. I have
labored for the poor gentleman to the extremest shore 255
of my modesty; but my brother justice have I found
so severe that he hath forced me to tell him he is indeed Justice.

Duke. If his own life answer the straitness of his
proceeding, it shall become him well; wherein if he 260
chance to fail, he hath sentenced himself.

Escal. I am going to visit the prisoner. Fare you
well.

Duke. Peace be with you!

             [Exeunt Escalus and Provost.]

    He who the sword of Heaven will bear   265
    Should be as holy as severe;

267. **Pattern in himself to know:** i.e., he should know himself to be the model on whom others will pattern their behavior.

272. **of his own liking:** similar to his own.

277. **likeness made in crimes:** i.e., the duplicating of Claudio's crime.

278. **Making practice on:** deceiving.

279. **To draw:** drawing.

Pattern in himself to know,
Grace to stand, and virtue go;
More nor less to others paying
Than by self-offenses weighing.   270
Shame to him whose cruel striking
Kills for faults of his own liking!
Twice treble shame on Angelo,
To weed my vice and let his grow!
O, what may man within him hide,   275
Though angel on the outward side!
How may likeness made in crimes,
Making practice on the times,
To draw with idle spiders' strings
Most ponderous and substantial things!   280
Craft against vice I must apply:
With Angelo tonight shall lie
His old betrothed but despised;
So disguise shall, by the disguised,
Pay with falsehood false exacting   285
And perform an old contracting.

Exit.

MEASURE
FOR
MEASURE

ACT IV

IV.i. The Duke visits Mariana and they are shortly joined by Isabella, who has made arrangements with Angelo and reports a plan to meet him in his garden in the middle of the night. The Duke introduces Mariana to Isabella, who tells her of the device for her to substitute at the rendezvous. Mariana agrees and the Duke assures her that she will not be committing a sin because Angelo is her husband by a pre-contract.

<hr />

10. **cry you mercy:** beg your pardon.
13. **My mirth it much displeased, but pleased my woe:** i.e., the music fed her grief rather than cheering her.

ACT IV

Scene I. [The moated grange at St. Luke's.]

Enter Mariana and Boy, singing.

Song.

Take, O, take those lips away,
   That so sweetly were forsworn;
And those eyes, the break of day,.
   Lights that do mislead the morn:
But my kisses bring again, bring again;   5
Seals of love, but sealed in vain, sealed in vain.
 Mar. Break off thy song and haste thee quick away.
Here comes a man of comfort, whose advice
Hath often stilled my brawling discontent.

                              [Exit Boy.]

Enter Duke [disguised].

I cry you mercy, sir, and well could wish   10
You had not found me here so musical.
Let me excuse me, and believe me so,
My mirth it much displeased, but pleased my woe.

22. **constantly:** firmly.

29. **circummured with brick:** surrounded by a brick wall.

31. **planched:** planked; made of wooden boards.

36. **heavy:** drowsy.

An Elizabethan garden. From Thomas Hill, *The Gardener's Labyrinth* (1577).

Duke. 'Tis good; though music oft hath such a
     charm   15
To make bad good and good provoke to harm.
I pray you, tell me, hath anybody inquired for me
     here today?
Much upon this time have I promised here to meet.
Mar. You have not been inquired after: I have sat   20
here all day.

Enter Isabella.

Duke. I do constantly believe you. The time is
come even now. I shall crave your forbearance a
little. May be I will call upon you anon, for some ad-
vantage to yourself.   25
Mar. I am always bound to you.   *Exit.*
Duke. Very well met, and well come.
What is the news from this good deputy?
Isa. He hath a garden circummured with brick,
Whose western side is with a vineyard backed;   30
And to that vineyard is a planched gate,
That makes his opening with this bigger key.
This other doth command a little door
Which from the vineyard to the garden leads.
There have I made my promise,   35
Upon the heavy middle of the night,
To call upon him.
Duke. But shall you on your knowledge find this
     way?
Isa. I have ta'en a due and wary note upon't: 40

[handwritten annotation: DRUNKEN PATH TO EDEN*]*

42. **In action all of precept:** instructing me by action.

45. **her observance:** i.e., that Mariana must observe.

47. **possessed:** informed.

50. **stays upon:** awaits; **whose persuasion is:** who has been led to believe that.

52. **borne up:** managed.

With whispering and most guilty diligence,
In action all of precept, he did show me
The way twice o'er.
   Duke. Are there no other tokens
Between you 'greed concerning her observance?   45
   Isa. No, none, but only a repair i' the dark;
And that I have possessed him my most stay
Can be but brief; for I have made him know
I have a servant comes with me along
That stays upon me, whose persuasion is   50
I come about my brother.
   Duke.   'Tis well borne up.
I have not yet made known to Mariana
A word of this. What, ho! within! come forth!

Enter Mariana.

I pray you, be acquainted with this maid;   55
She comes to do you good.
   Isa.   I do desire the like.
   Duke. Do you persuade yourself that I respect you?
   Mar. Good friar, I know you do and have found it.
   Duke. Take, then, this your companion by the   60
     hand,
Who hath a story ready for your ear.
I shall attend your leisure, but make haste;
The vaporous night approaches.
   Mar. Will't please you walk aside?   65
               [Exeunt Mariana and Isabella.]
   Duke. O place and greatness, millions of false eyes

67. **stuck:** fixed.

68. **contrarious quests:** hostile speculations.

69. **escapes:** sallies.

71. **rack:** distort.

83. **To bring you thus together, 'tis no sin:** the Duke contradicts the attitude he has expressed, in his friar's disguise, toward the cohabitation of Claudio and Juliet, who were also betrothed on a pre-contract. But the point of view expressed here may be intended as the Duke's true attitude, while the previous one was essential to his role as a religious adviser. In any case, absolute ethical consistency is incompatible with the requirements of Shakespeare's plot, which diverges from his sources in having Isabella escape dishonor by means of the substitution, while the heroine in the sources submitted.

85. **flourish:** embellish.

Are stuck upon thee! volumes of report
Run with these false and most contrarious quests
Upon thy doings! thousand escapes of wit
<u>Make thee the father of their idle dream,</u>   ○   70
And rack thee in their fancies!

       Enter Mariana and Isabella.

                 Welcome, how agreed?
   Isa. She'll take the enterprise upon her, father,
If you advise it.
   Duke.   It is not my consent,   75
But my entreaty too.
   Isa.   Little have you to say
When you depart from him, but, soft and low,
"Remember now my brother."
   Mar.   Fear me not.   80
   Duke. Nor, gentle daughter, fear you not at all.
He is your husband on a pre-contract:
To bring you thus together, 'tis no sin,
Sith that the justice of your title to him
Doth flourish the deceit. Come, let us go.   85
Our corn's to reap, for yet our tithe's to sow.

                     Exeunt.

IV.ii. The provost suggests that Pompey become executioner's assistant for two executions scheduled for the following day: Claudio and Barnardine. Abhorson, the executioner, and Pompey agree. The provost shows Claudio the warrant for his death. The Duke comes to inquire whether Claudio has received a reprieve. While he waits, a message from Angelo arrives, but contrary to the Duke's expectation it is an order for Claudio to be executed by four o'clock no matter what may come. The Duke, promising to prove in four days' time that Angelo is guilty of the same sin for which he would kill Claudio, obtains a stay of execution. He suggests that the provost send the head of Barnardine to Angelo to conceal the delay.

▐▊▌▊▐▊▌▊▐▊▌▊▐▊▌▊▐▊▌▊▐▊▌▊▐▊

6. **snatches:** quibbles.
11. **gyves:** fetters.
13. **unpitied:** pitiless.

Whipping at the cart's tail, the common punishment for whores, vagabonds, and similar offenders. From Thomas Harman, *A . . . Warning for Common Cursitors* (1567).

Scene II. [A room in the prison.]

Enter Provost and Clown [Pompey].

Pro. Come hither, sirrah. Can you cut off a man's head?

Pom. If the man be a bachelor, sir, I can; but if he be a married man, he's his wife's head, and I can never cut off a woman's head.   5

Pro. Come, sir, leave me your snatches and yield me a direct answer. Tomorrow morning are to die Claudio and Barnardine. Here is in our prison a common executioner, who in his office lacks a helper. If you will take it on you to assist him, it shall redeem   10 you from your gyves. If not, you shall have your full time of imprisonment and your deliverance with an unpitied whipping, for you have been a notorious bawd.

Pom. Sir, I have been an unlawful bawd time out of   15 mind; but yet I will be content to be a lawful hangman. I would be glad to receive some instruction from my fellow partner.

Pro. What, ho! Abhorson! Where's Abhorson, there?   20

Enter Abhorson.

Abhor. Do you call, sir?
Pro. Sirrah, here's a fellow will help you tomorrow

23–24. **compound with him by the year:** agree on terms for a year's service with him.

26. **plead his estimation:** urge his reputation in discussing terms.

29. **mystery:** profession; craft.

32–33. **favor . . . favor:** indulgence . . . face.

43. **true:** honest. Abhorson argues that a thief is like a tailor (a member of a respectable craft) in that he fits himself into any honest man's clothing. Likewise the hangman fits himself to the clothing of any executed thief and thus practices the same craft.

in your execution. If you think it meet, compound
with him by the year and let him abide here with you;
if not, use him for the present and dismiss him. He   25
cannot plead his estimation with you: he hath been a
bawd.

Abhor. A bawd, sir? Fie upon him! he will discredit
our mystery.

Pro. Go to, sir: you weigh equally: a feather will   30
turn the scale.   *Exit.*

Pom. Pray, sir, by your good favor—for surely, sir,
a good favor you have, but that you have a hanging
look—do you call, sir, your occupation a mystery?

Abhor. Ay, sir, a mystery.   35

Pom. Painting, sir, I have heard say, is a mystery;
and your whores, sir, being members of my occupation, using painting, do prove my occupation a
mystery: but what mystery there should be in hanging, if I should be hanged, I cannot imagine.   40

Abhor. Sir, it is a mystery.

Pom. Proof?

Abhor. Every true man's apparel fits your thief. If
it be too little for your thief, your true man thinks it
big enough. If it be too big for your thief, your thief   45
thinks it little enough. So every true man's apparel
fits your thief.

SAVIOR shall come as a thief in the night

Enter Provost.

Pro. Are you agreed?

Pom. Sir, I will serve him; for I do find your hang-

51. **ask forgiveness:** i.e., of the condemned man before execution.

57. **turn:** hanging. The executioner was said to "turn off" a prisoner when he hanged him.

58. **yare:** quick and deft.

73. **By and by:** "I'm coming," addressed to the one who knocks.

HANGING - EJACULATION

man is a more penitent trade than your bawd: he 50
doth oftener ask <u>forgiveness</u>.

Pro. You, sirrah, provide your block and your ax
tomorrow four o'clock.

Abhor. Come on, bawd, I will instruct thee in my
trade: follow. 55

Pom. I do desire to learn, sir: and I hope, if you
have occasion to use me for your own turn, you shall
find me yare; for, truly, sir, for your kindness I owe
you a good turn.

Pro. Call hither Barnardine and Claudio: 60
               Exeunt [Pompey and Abhorson].
Th' one has my pity; not a jot the other,
Being a murderer, though he were my brother.

Enter Claudio.

Look, here's the warrant, Claudio, for thy death:
'Tis now dead midnight, and by eight tomorrow
Thou must be made immortal. Where's Barnardine? 65

Claud. As fast locked up in sleep as guiltless labor
When it lies starkly in the traveler's bones.
He will not wake.

Pro.   Who can do good on him?
Well, go, prepare yourself.   *[Knocking within.]* 70
          But, hark, what noise?—
Heaven give your spirits comfort!   *[Exit Claudio.]*
              By and by!—
I hope it is some pardon or reprieve
For the most gentle Claudio. 75

88. **stroke and line:** i.e., the standard he observes in administering justice.

91. **qualify:** temper; subdue; **mealed:** stained.

96. **steeled:** hardened.

99. **unsisting:** unresisting.

Enter Duke [disguised].

                    Welcome, father.
Duke. The best and wholesomest spirits of the
  night
Envelop you, good provost! Who called here of late?
Pro. None, since the curfew rung.   80
Duke. Not Isabel?
Pro. No.
Duke. They will, then, ere't be long.
Pro. What comfort is for Claudio?
Duke. There's some in hope.   85
Pro.   It is a bitter deputy.
Duke. Not so, not so: his life is paralleled
Even with the stroke and line of his great justice.
He doth with holy abstinence subdue
That in himself which he spurs on his power   90
To qualify in others. Were he mealed with that
Which he corrects, then were he tyrannous;
But this being so, he's just.   [*Knocking within.*]
                    Now are they come.
                          [*Exit Provost.*]
This is a gentle provost: seldom when   95
The steeled jailer is the friend of men.
                          [*Knocking within.*]
How now! what noise? That spirit's possessed with
  haste
That wounds the unsisting postern with these strokes.

          [*Enter Provost.*]

107. **Happily:** perhaps.
110. **siege:** seat.

Pro. There he must stay until the officer 100
Arise to let him in: he is called up.

Duke. Have you no countermand for Claudio yet,
But he must die tomorrow?

Pro.   None, sir, none.

Duke. As near the dawning, provost, as it is, 105
You shall hear more ere morning.

Pro.   Happily
You something know. Yet I believe there comes
No countermand: no such example have we.
Besides, upon the very siege of justice 110
Lord Angelo hath to the public ear
Professed the contrary.

Enter a Messenger.

                    This is His Lordship's man.

Duke. And here comes Claudio's pardon.

Mess. [*Giving a paper*] My lord hath sent you this 115
note; and by me this further charge, that you swerve
not from the smallest article of it, neither in time,
matter, or other circumstance. Good morrow; for, as
I take it, it is almost day.

Pro. I shall obey him.   [*Exit Messenger.*] 120

Duke. [*Aside*] This is his pardon, purchased by
    such sin
For which the pardoner himself is in.
Hence hath offense his quick celerity,
When it is borne in high authority. 125
When vice makes mercy, mercy's so extended,

129. **belike:** perhaps.

131. **putting-on:** urging.

139. **deliver:** report.

145. **a prisoner nine years old:** i.e., nine years a prisoner.

150. **fact:** crime.

That for the fault's love is the offender friended.
Now, sir, what news?

Pro. I told you. Lord Angelo, belike thinking me
remiss in mine office, awakens me with this unwonted 130
putting-on; methinks strangely, for he hath not used it
before.

Duke. Pray you, let's hear.

Pro. [*Reads*]

The Letter.

"Whatsoever you may hear to the contrary, le̲
Claudio be executed by four of the clock; and in the 135
afternoon Barnardine. For my better satisfaction, let
me have Claudio's head sent me by five. Let this be
duly performed, with a thought that more depends on
it than we must yet deliver. Thus fail not to do your
office, as you will answer it at your peril."   140
What say you to this, sir?

Duke. What is that Barnardine who is to be executed in the afternoon?

Pro. A Bohemian born, but here nursed up and
bred; one that is a prisoner nine years old.   145

Duke. How came it that the absent Duke had not
either delivered him to his liberty or executed him? I
have heard it was ever his manner to do so.

Pro. His friends still wrought reprieves for him:
and, indeed, his fact, till now in the government of 150
Lord Angelo, came not to an undoubtful proof.

Duke. It is now apparent?

Pro. Most manifest, and not denied by himself.

159. **desperately mortal:** utterly unmindful of death.

163. **Drunk many times a day:** prisons of the time were very different from those of today. Instead of being boarded at the state's expense, prisoners could buy any food or other comforts they could afford. If they had no money, they had no privileges, and were often forced to beg through the prison bars for their very food.

169–70. **in the boldness of my cunning:** relying boldly on my knowledge.

173–74. **in a manifested effect:** by unmistakable evidence.

183. **warrant you:** assure you of safety.

Duke. Hath he borne himself penitently in prison?
How seems he to be touched?   155

Pro. A man that apprehends death no more dread-
fully but as a <u>drunken sleep:</u> careless, reckless, and
fearless of what's past, present, or to come; insensible
of mortality, and desperately mortal.

Duke. He wants advice.   160

Pro. He will hear none. He hath evermore had the
liberty of the prison: give him leave to escape hence,
he would not. Drunk many times a day, if not many
days entirely drunk. We have very oft awaked him,
as if to carry him to execution, and showed him a   165
seeming warrant for it: it hath not moved him at all.

Duke. More of him anon. There is written in your
brow, provost, honesty and constancy. If I read it not
truly, my ancient skill beguiles me; in the boldness of
my cunning, I will lay myself in hazard. Claudio,   170
whom here you have warrant to execute, is no greater
forfeit to the law than Angelo who hath sentenced
him. To make you understand this in a manifested
effect, I crave but four days' respite; for the which
you are to do me both a present and a dangerous   175
courtesy.

Pro. Pray, sir, in what?

Duke. In the delaying death.

Pro. Alack, how may I do it, having the hour
limited and an express command, under penalty, to   180
deliver his head in the view of Angelo? I may make
my case as Claudio's, to cross this in the smallest.

Duke. By the vow of mine order I warrant you, if

187–88. **discover the favor:** recognize the face.

193. **fall to you:** befall you.

194. **profess:** profess allegiance to (the founder of his order).

208. **character:** handwriting.

my instructions may be your guide. Let this Barnardine be this morning executed and his head borne   185
to Angelo.

Pro. Angelo hath seen them both, and will discover
the favor.

Duke. O, death's a great disguiser; and you may
add to it. Shave the head and tie the beard, and say it   190
was the desire of the penitent to be so bared before
his death. You know the course is common. If anything fall to you upon this more than thanks and
good fortune, by the saint whom I profess, I will
plead against it with my life.   195

Pro. Pardon me, good father, it is against my oath.

Duke. Were you sworn to the Duke or to the
deputy?

Pro. To him and to his substitutes.

Duke. You will think you have made no offense, if   200
the Duke avouch the justice of your dealing?

Pro. But what likelihood is in that?

Duke. Not a resemblance, but a certainty. Yet
since I see you fearful, that neither my coat, integrity,
nor persuasion can with ease attempt you, I will go   205
further than I meant, to pluck all fears out of you.
Look you, sir, here is the hand and seal of the Duke.
You know the character, I doubt not, and the signet is
not strange to you.

Pro. I know them both.   210

Duke. The contents of this is the return of the
Duke. You shall anon overread it at your pleasure;
where you shall find, within these two days he will be

218. the unfolding star calls up the shepherd: the morning star signals the shepherd to lead forth his flock.

222. give him a present shrift: hear his confession and give him absolution immediately.

224. resolve: satisfy.

<hr>

IV.iii. When Abhorson summons Barnardine to his execution, the latter replies that he has been drinking all night and is not prepared to die. Since they are unwilling to send a man to death unprepared, the provost suggests that they substitute the head of the pirate Ragozine, who died that morning of a fever. The Duke now proposes to write to Angelo reporting his own unexpected return, with directions for Angelo to meet him near the city. When Isabella comes to satisfy herself of her brother's safety, the Duke reports his execution. Isabella threatens to retaliate, but the Duke counsels patience. The indiscreet Lucio, seeking news of Claudio, voices more slanderous gossip about the supposedly absent Duke.

<hr>

5. commodity: lot. Master Rash's offense was participation in a transaction with a moneylender, who supplied him with a **commodity** on credit, for which he ultimately paid a price far in excess of the value of the goods, thus attempting to circumvent the statutes limiting the interest rates on loans to 10 per cent; **ginger:** a favorite tidbit for old women to chew.

here. This is a thing that Angelo knows not; for he
this very day receives letters of strange tenor, per- 215
chance of the Duke's death, perchance entering into
some monastery; but, by chance, nothing of what is
writ. Look, the unfolding star calls up the shepherd.
Put not yourself into amazement how these things
should be: all difficulties are but easy when they are 220
known. Call your executioner, and off with Barnardine's head. I will give him a present shrift and advise him for a better place. Yet you are amazed; but
this shall absolutely resolve you. Come away; it is
almost clear dawn. 225

Exeunt.

Scene III. [Another room in the prison.]

Enter Clown [Pompey].

Pom. I am as well acquainted here as I was in our
house of profession. One would think it were Mistress
Overdone's own house, for here be many of her old
customers. First, here's young Master Rash: he's in
for a commodity of brown paper and old ginger, nine- 5
score and seventeen pounds; of which he made five
marks ready money. Marry, then ginger was not much
in request, for the old women were all dead. Then is
there here one Master Caper, at the suit of Master
Threepile the mercer, for some four suits of peach- 10

11. **peaches:** impeaches.

19. **are now "for the Lord's sake":** an allusion to the fact that moneyless prisoners were forced to beg for their livings from passers-by. "For the Lord's sake" was a typical beggar's phrase.

colored satin, which now peaches him a beggar. Then
have we here young Dizie, and young Master Deep-
vow, and Master Copperspur, and Master Starve-
lackey the rapier and dagger man, and young
Dropheir that killed lusty Pudding, and Master 15
Forthright the tilter, and brave Master Shootie the
great traveler, and wild Halfcan that stabbed Pots,
and, I think, forty more—all great doers in our trade,
and are now "for the Lord's sake."

Enter Abhorson.

Abhor. Sirrah, bring Barnardine hither. 20
Pom. Master Barnardine! you must rise and be
hanged, Master Barnardine!
Abhor. What, ho, Barnardine!
Bar. [*Within*] A pox o' your throats! Who makes
that noise there? What are you? 25
Pom. Your friends, sir; the hangman. You must be
so good, sir, to rise and be put to death.
Bar. [*Within*] Away, you rogue, away! I am sleepy.
Abhor. Tell him he must awake, and that quickly
too. 30
Pom. Pray, Master Barnardine, awake till you are
executed, and sleep afterwards.
Abhor. Go in to him, and fetch him out.
Pom. He is coming, sir, he is coming. I hear his
straw rustle. 35
Abhor. Is the ax upon the block, sirrah?
Pom. Very ready, sir.

40. **clap into:** set about briskly.
45. **betimes:** early.
47–48. **ghostly father:** confessor.
54. **billets:** pieces of wood.

The condemned prisoner says his last farewells. From the Roxburghe Ballads, a collection of seventeenth-century broadside ballads reprinted 1871-99.

Enter Barnardine.

Bar. How now, Abhorson? What's the news with
you?

Abhor. Truly, sir, I would desire you to clap into   40
your prayers; for, look you, the warrant's come.

Bar. You rogue, I have been drinking all night: I
am not fitted for't.

Pom. O, the better, sir; for he that drinks all night
and is hanged betimes in the morning may sleep the   45
sounder all the next day.

Abhor. Look you, sir, here comes your ghostly
father. Do we jest now, think you?

Enter Duke [disguised].

Duke. Sir, induced by my charity, and hearing how
hastily you are to depart, I am come to advise you,   50
comfort you, and pray with you.

Bar. Friar, not I: I have been drinking hard all
night, and I will have more time to prepare me, or
they shall beat out my brains with billets. I will not
consent to die this day, that's certain.   55

Duke. O, sir, you must: and therefore I beseech
   you,
Look forward on the journey you shall go.

Bar. I swear I will not die today for any man's
persuasion.   60

Duke. But hear you.

74. **omit:** let go; allow to live.
78. **accident:** happening.
79. **presently:** at once.

Bar. Not a word! If you have anything to say to me,
come to my ward; for thence will not I today.   *Exit.*

Duke. Unfit to live or die. O gravel heart!
After him, fellows; bring him to the block.   65
                    [*Exeunt Abhorson and Pompey.*]

                    Enter Provost.

Pro. Now, sir, how do you find the prisoner?

Duke. A creature unprepared, unmeet for death;
And to transport him in the mind he is
Were damnable.

Pro.   Here in the prison, father,   70
There died this morning of a cruel fever
One Ragozine, a most notorious pirate,
A man of Claudio's years, his beard and head
Just of his color. What if we do omit
This reprobate till he were well inclined   75
And satisfy the deputy with the visage
Of Ragozine, more like to Claudio?

Duke. O, 'tis an accident that Heaven provides!
Dispatch it presently: the hour draws on
Prefixed by Angelo. See this be done   80
And sent according to command, whiles I
Persuade this rude wretch willingly to die.

Pro. This shall be done, good father, presently.
But Barnardine must die this afternoon.
And how shall we continue Claudio,   85
To save me from the danger that might come
If he were known alive?

91. **journal:** daily.

92. **the under generation:** the people of the Antipodes, on the other side of the world.

94. **your free dependant:** freely at your service.

104. **by cold gradation:** by degrees, slowly and carefully.

Duke. Let this be done.
Put them in secret holds, both Barnardine
And Claudio.   90
Ere twice the sun hath made his journal greeting
To the under generation, you shall find
Your safety manifested.
    Pro. I am your free dependant.
    Duke. Quick, dispatch, and send the head to   95
    Angelo.   *Exit* [*Provost*].
Now will I write letters to Angelo—
The provost, he shall bear them—whose contents
Shall witness to him I am near at home,
And that, by great injunctions, I am bound   100
To enter publicly. Him I'll desire
To meet me at the consecrated fount,
A league below the city; and from thence,
By cold gradation and well-balanced form,
We shall proceed with Angelo.   105

Enter Provost.

    Pro. Here is the head. I'll carry it myself.
    Duke. Convenient is it. Make a swift return;
For I would commune with you of such things
That want no ear but yours.
    Pro.   I'll make all speed. *Exit.* 110
    Isa. [*Within*] Peace, ho, be here!
    Duke. The tongue of Isabel. She's come to know
If yet her brother's pardon be come hither:
But I will keep her ignorant of her good,

127. **In your close patience:** i.e., by enduring Angelo's treachery silently.

132. **nor:** neither.

137. **covent:** convent.

138. **instance:** information.

To make her heavenly comforts of despair   115
When it is least expected.

Enter Isabella.

Isa.   Ho, by your leave!

Duke. Good morning to you, fair and gracious
    daughter.

Isa. The better, given me by so holy a man.   120

Hath yet the deputy sent my brother's pardon?

Duke. He hath released him, Isabel, from the
    world:

His head is off and sent to Angelo.

Isa. Nay, but it is not so.   125

Duke. It is no other: show your wisdom, daughter,

In your close patience.

Isa. O, I will to him and pluck out his eyes! *✓eye for an*

Duke. You shall not be admitted to his sight. *offending eye*

Isa. Unhappy Claudio! wretched Isabel!   130

Injurious world! most damned Angelo!

Duke. This nor hurts him nor profits you a jot;

Forbear it therefore: give your cause to Heaven.

Mark what I say, which you shall find

By every syllable a faithful verity.   135

The Duke comes home tomorrow—nay, dry your eyes!

One of our covent and his confessor

Gives me this instance. Already he hath carried

Notice to Escalus and Angelo,

Who do prepare to meet him at the gates,   140

144. **bosom:** heart's desire.
152. **perfect him withal:** inform him in full.
154. **home and home:** to the utmost.
155. **combined:** pledged.
157. **fretting:** irritating.
163. **fain:** obliged.

There to give up their pow'r. If you can, pace your
    wisdom
In that good path that I would wish it go,
And you shall have your bosom on this wretch,
Grace of the Duke, revenges to your heart,   145
And general honor.

  Isa.   I am directed by you.

  Duke. This letter, then, to Friar Peter give:
'Tis that he sent me of the Duke's return.
Say, by this token, I desire his company   150
At Mariana's house tonight. Her cause and yours
I'll perfect him withal; and he shall bring you
Before the Duke; and to the head of Angelo
Accuse him home and home. For my poor self,
I am combined by a sacred vow,   155
And shall be absent. Wend you with this letter.
Command these fretting waters from your eyes
With a light heart. Trust not my holy order
If I pervert your course—Who's here?

Enter Lucio.

  Lucio. Good even. Friar, where's the provost?   160
  Duke. Not within, sir.
  Lucio. O pretty Isabella, I am pale at mine heart to
see thine eyes so red. Thou must be patient. I am fain
to dine and sup with water and bran. I dare not for
my head fill my belly; one fruitful meal would set me 165
to't. But they say the Duke will be here tomorrow.

167–68. **old fantastical:** very whimsical.

168. **of dark corners:** given to secret trysts with women.

171. **he lives not in them:** they do not depict him accurately.

173. **woodman:** huntsman; i.e., pursuer of women.

185. **medlar:** a fruit eaten when rotten.

186. **fairer:** more genial.

By my troth, Isabel, I loved thy brother. If the old fantastical Duke of dark corners had been at home, he had lived. [*Exit Isabella.*]

Duke. Sir, the Duke is marvelous little beholding 170 to your reports; but the best is, he lives not in them.

Lucio. Friar, thou knowest not the Duke so well as I do: he's a better woodman than thou takest him for.

Duke. Well, you'll answer this one day. Fare ye well. 175

Lucio. Nay, tarry; I'll go along with thee. I can tell thee pretty tales of the Duke.

Duke. You have told me too many of him already, sir, if they be true; if not true, none were enough.

Lucio. I was once before him for getting a wench 180 with child.

Duke. Did you such a thing?

Lucio. Yes, marry, did I: but I was fain to forswear it; they would else have married me to the rotten medlar. 185

Duke. Sir, your company is fairer than honest. Rest you well.

Lucio. By my troth, I'll go with thee to the lane's end. If bawdy talk offend you, we'll have very little of it. Nay, friar, I am a kind of burr; I shall stick. 190

Exeunt.

IV.iv. Angelo and Escalus puzzle over contradictory letters received from the Duke. Angelo is worried lest Isabella denounce him. He believes, however, that he is safe and regrets that he had to execute Claudio to protect his own reputation.

||||||||||||||||||||||||||||||||||||

1. **disvouched:** contradicted.
12. **devices:** plots.
17. **sort and suit:** suitable rank.
21. **unshapes:** destroys; **unpregnant:** disinclined; unready.

Scene IV. [A room in Angelo's house.]

Enter Angelo and Escalus.

Escal. Every letter he hath writ hath disvouched other.

Ang. In most uneven and distracted manner. His actions show much like to madness: pray Heaven his wisdom be not tainted! And why meet him at the 5
gates and redeliver our authorities there?

Escal. I guess not.

Ang. And why should we proclaim it in an hour before his ent'ring that if any crave redress of injustice they should exhibit their petitions in the street? 10

Escal. He shows his reason for that: to have a dispatch of complaints, and to deliver us from devices hereafter, which shall then have no power to stand against us.

Ang. Well, I beseech you let it be proclaimed. 15
Betimes i' the morn I'll call you at your house.
Give notice to such men of sort and suit
As are to meet him.

Escal.   I shall, sir. Fare you well.   *Exit.*

Ang. Good night. 20
This deed unshapes me quite, makes me unpregnant
And dull to all proceedings. A deflowered maid!
And by an eminent body that enforced
The law against it! But that her tender shame
Will not proclaim against her maiden loss, 25

26. **tongue:** denounce; **dares her no:** makes her fear to do so.

27. **bears of a credent bulk:** carries such a weight of credibility.

28. **That:** so that; **particular:** personal.

29. **confounds:** destroys; **breather:** utterer.

IV.v. The Duke, no longer disguised, gives letters to Friar Peter to deliver to various men in Vienna.

1. **deliver me:** deliver for me.
4. **drift:** intention.
5. **blench:** shy away; deviate.
9. **trumpets:** trumpeters.

How might she tongue me! Yet reason dares her no;
For my authority bears of a credent bulk,
That no particular scandal once can touch
But it confounds the breather. He should have lived,
Save that his riotous youth, with dangerous sense,   30
Might in the times to come have ta'en revenge,
By so receiving a dishonored life
With ransom of such shame. Would yet he had lived!
Alack, when once our grace we have forgot,
Nothing goes right: we would, and we would not.   35
                                              Exit.

Scene V. [Fields without the town.]

Enter Duke, [in his own habit,] and Friar Peter.

Duke. These letters at fit time deliver me.
The provost knows our purpose and our plot.
The matter being afoot, keep your instruction
And hold you ever to our special drift;
Though sometimes you do blench from this to that   5
As cause doth minister. Go call at Flavius' house
And tell him where I stay. Give the like notice
To Valentius, Rowland, and to Crassus,
And bid them bring the trumpets to the gate;
But send me Flavius first.   10
    Friar.   It shall be speeded well.
                                              [*Exit.*]

IV.vi. Isabella, Mariana, and Friar Peter approach the city gates. They have been advised by the disguised Duke to wait there for their chance to accuse Angelo.

᠁᠁᠁᠁᠁᠁᠁᠁᠁᠁᠁᠁

1. **indirectly:** untruthfully.
4. **veil full purpose:** conceal our ultimate plan.

Enter Varrius.

Duke. I thank thee, Varrius. Thou hast made good
   haste.
Come, we will walk. There's other of our friends
Will greet us here anon, my gentle Varrius.   15
                          Exeunt.

Scene VI. [Street near the city gate.]

Enter Isabella and Mariana.

Isa. To speak so indirectly I am loath.
I would say the truth; but to accuse him so,
That is your part. Yet I am advised to do it;
He says, to veil full purpose.
Mar.   Be ruled by him.   5
Isa. Besides, he tells me that if peradventure
He speak against me on the adverse side,
I should not think it strange, for 'tis a physic
That's bitter to sweet end.

Enter [Friar] Peter.

Mar. I would Friar Peter—   10
Isa.   O peace! the friar is come.
Friar. Come, I have found you out a stand most fit,

16. **generous and gravest:** noblest and most dignified.

17. **hent:** literally, "seized upon"; i.e., preempted for their stations.

Where you may have such vantage on the Duke
He shall not pass you. Twice have the trumpets
    sounded.   15
The generous and gravest citizens
Have hent the gates, and very near upon
The Duke is ent'ring: therefore, hence, away!

                        Exeunt.

MEASURE
FOR
MEASURE

ACT V

V.i. Duke Vincentio is greeted at the gates by Angelo and Escalus, to whom he gives fulsome praise for their government in his absence. Isabella then comes forward and denounces Angelo. The Duke pretends to regard her as demented or bribed to accuse his deputy falsely. She mentions the name of Friar Lodowick, the Duke's alias, and Lucio professes to know him, describing him as a saucy fellow who slandered the Duke. Friar Peter produces Mariana, who reveals that Angelo spent the previous night in her arms. Angelo admits that he was once betrothed to Mariana but denies having seen her during the past five years. The Duke charges Mariana with complicity in a plot to discredit Angelo and orders Escalus and Angelo to decide the matter while Friar Lodowick is sought to tell his story. The Duke leaves and shortly returns in his friar's disguise. Escalus charges him of having arranged the plot against Angelo and threatens him with the rack. Lucio repeats his accusation that the friar has slandered the Duke and pulls off his hood, revealing the Duke himself. Ashamed that the Duke knows the story of his villainy, Angelo begs for immediate death, but the Duke orders that he first marry Mariana. He urges Isabella to forgive Angelo but decrees that (Contd. on p. 92)

‖‖‖‖‖‖‖‖‖‖‖‖‖‖‖‖‖‖‖‖‖‖‖‖‖‖‖

8. **Forerunning more requital:** anticipating additional reward.

12. **covert:** hidden.

14. **forted:** fortified.

ACT V

Scene I. [The city gate.]

[*Mariana veiled, Isabella, and Friar Peter at their
stand.*] *Enter Duke, Varrius, Lords, Angelo, Escalus,
Lucio,* [*Provost, Officers, and*] *Citizens, at several
doors.*

Duke. My very worthy cousin, fairly met!
Our old and faithful friend, we are glad to see you.

Ang. } Happy return be to your royal Grace!
Escal.

Duke. Many and hearty thankings to you both.
We have made inquiry of you, and we hear   5
Such goodness of your justice that our soul
Cannot but yield you forth to public thanks,
Forerunning more requital.

Ang.   You make my bonds still greater.

Duke. O, your desert speaks loud; and I should   10
    wrong it
To lock it in the wards of covert bosom,
When it deserves with characters of brass
A forted residence 'gainst the tooth of time
And razure of oblivion. Give me your hand,   15
And let the subject see, to make them know

91

Angelo must pay with his life for the death of Claudio. Mariana pleads for his husband's life, and Isabella adds her own importunities, arguing that her brother was executed for a crime he had indeed committed. At length the provost discloses that he has spared Barnardine, whom the Duke pardons, and produces Claudio alive, whom the Duke also pardons for Isabella's "lovely sake." Pleased with Isabella, the Duke asks her hand. He forgives Angelo and turns his attention to Lucio, whom he finds it harder to forgive, but he at last orders him to marry the prostitute who has borne him a child.

‖‖‖‖‖‖‖‖‖‖‖‖‖‖‖‖‖‖‖‖‖‖‖‖‖‖‖‖‖‖‖

23. **Vail your regard:** lower your glance.

That outward courtesies would fain proclaim
Favors that keep within. Come, Escalus;
You must walk by us on our other hand:
And good supporters are you.   20

[*Friar Peter and Isabella come forward.*]

Friar. Now is your time: speak loud, and kneel be-
fore him.
Isa. Justice, O royal Duke! Vail your regard
Upon a wronged, I would fain have said, a maid!
O worthy prince, dishonor not your eye   25
By throwing it on any other object
Till you have heard me in my true complaint,
And given me justice, justice, justice, justice!
Duke. Relate your wrongs; in what? by whom? Be
   brief.   30
Here is Lord Angelo shall give you justice:
Reveal yourself to him.
Isa.   O worthy Duke,
You bid me seek redemption of the Devil.
Hear me yourself; for that which I must speak   35
Must either punish me, not being believed,
Or wring redress from you. Hear me, O hear me, here!
Ang. My lord, her wits, I fear me, are not firm.
She hath been a suitor to me for her brother
Cut off by course of justice—   40
Isa.   By course of justice!
Ang. And she will speak most bitterly and strange.
Isa. Most strange, but yet most truly, will I speak.

SATAN - prosecutor in Jehova's COURT

62. **caitiff:** villain.
63. **absolute:** perfect.
65. **dressings:** trimmings; **caracts:** insignia.

That Angelo's forsworn; is it not strange?
That Angelo's a murderer; is't not strange?   45
That Angelo is an adulterous thief,
An hypocrite, a virgin-violator;
Is it not strange and strange?
 Duke.   Nay, it is ten times strange.
 Isa. It is not truer he is <u>Angelo</u>   50
Than this is all as true as it is strange.
Nay, it is ten times true; for truth is truth
To the end of reck'ning.
 Duke.   Away with her!—Poor soul,
She speaks this in the infirmity of sense.   55
 Isa. O prince, I conjure thee, as thou believest
There is another comfort than this world,
That thou neglect me not with that opinion
That I am touched with madness! Make not im-
  possible   60
That which but seems unlike. 'Tis not impossible
But one, the wicked'st caitiff on the ground,
May seem as shy, as grave, as just, as absolute
As Angelo. Even so may Angelo,
In all his dressings, caracts, titles, forms,   65
Be an archvillain. Believe it, royal Prince!
<u>If he be less, he's nothing</u>; but he's more,
Had I more name for badness.
 Duke.   By mine honesty,
If she be mad—as I believe no other—   70
Her madness hath the oddest frame of sense,
Such a dependency of thing on thing,
As e'er I heard in madness.

78. **seems:** i.e., that seems.
87. **and't like:** if it please.
98. **perfect:** completely honest.

    Isa.   O gracious Duke,
Harp not on that; nor do not banish reason   75
For inequality, but let your reason serve
To make the truth appear where it seems hid
And hide the false seems true.
    Duke.   Many that are not mad
Have, sure, more lack of reason. What would you say?   80
    Isa. I am the sister of one Claudio,
Condemned upon the act of fornication
To lose his head; condemned by Angelo.
I, in probation of a sisterhood,
Was sent to by my brother; one Lucio   85
As then the messenger—
    Lucio.   That's I, and't like your Grace:
I came to her from Claudio, and desired her
To try her gracious fortune with Lord Angelo
For her poor brother's pardon.   90
    Isa.   That's he indeed.
    Duke. You were not bid to speak.
    Lucio.   No, my good lord;
Nor wished to hold my peace.
    Duke.   I wish you now, then: 95
Pray you, take note of it; and when you have
A business for yourself, pray Heaven you then
Be perfect.
    Lucio. I warrant your Honor.
    Duke. The warrant's for yourself: take heed to't.   100
    Isa. This gentleman told somewhat of my tale—
    Lucio. Right.

109. **to the matter:** to the point; apt.

111. **needless process:** nonessential part of the story.

113. **refelled:** repulsed.

119. **remorse:** compassion.

124. **like:** probable; plausible (so as to be convincing).

125. **fond:** foolish.

127. **suborned:** bribed.

128. **practice:** plot.

129. **imports:** carries with it.

Duke. It may be right; but you are i' the wrong
To speak before your time. Proceed.
Isa.   I went   105
To this pernicious caitiff deputy—
    Duke. That's somewhat madly spoken.
    Isa.   Pardon it!
The phrase is to the matter.
    Duke. Mended again. The matter—proceed.   110
    Isa. In brief—to set the needless process by,
How I persuaded, how I prayed and kneeled,
How he refelled me, and how I replied—
For this was of much length—the vile conclusion
I now begin with grief and shame to utter: 115
He would not, but by gift of my chaste body
To his concupiscible intemperate lust,
Release my brother; and after much debatement
My sisterly remorse confutes mine honor,
And I did yield to him: but the next morn betimes, 120
His purpose surfeiting, he sends a warrant
For my poor brother's head.
    Duke.   This is most likely!
    Isa. O, that it were as like as it is true!
    Duke. By Heaven, fond wretch, thou knowst not 125
        what thou speakst,
Or else thou art suborned against his honor
In hateful practice. First, his integrity
Stands without blemish. Next, it imports no reason
That with such vehemency he should pursue   130
Faults proper to himself. If he had so offended,
He would have weighed thy brother by himself,

139–40. **wrapt up/In countenance:** protected by official sanction.

153. **swinged:** beaten.

154. **This':** a contraction of "this is."

159. **scurvy:** contemptible.

162. **abused:** wronged by falsehood.

And not have cut him off. Someone hath set you on.
Confess the truth and say by whose advice
Thou camest here to complain.   135
  Isa.   And is this all?
Then, O you blessed ministers above,
Keep me in patience and with ripened time
Unfold the evil which is here wrapt up
In countenance!—Heaven shield your Grace from woe,   140
As I, thus wronged, hence unbelieved go!
  Duke. I know you'ld fain be gone.—An officer!
To prison with her!—Shall we thus permit
A blasting and a scandalous breath to fall
On him so near us? This needs must be a practice.   145
Who knew of your intent and coming hither?
  Isa. One that I would were here, Friar Lodowick.
  Duke. A ghostly father, belike. Who knows that
Lodowick?
  Lucio. My lord, I know him: 'tis a meddling friar.   150
I do not like the man. Had he been lay, my lord,
For certain words he spake against your Grace
In your retirement I had swinged him soundly.
  Duke. Words against me! This' a good friar, belike!
And to set on this wretched woman here   155
Against our substitute! Let this friar be found.
  Lucio. But yesternight, my lord, she and that friar,
I saw them at the prison: a saucy friar,
A very scurvy fellow.
  Friar. Blessed be your royal Grace!   160
I have stood by, my lord, and I have heard
Your royal ear abused. First hath this woman

165. **As she from one ungot:** as she differs from an unborn child.

169. **temporary meddler:** meddler in worldly affairs.

176. **mere:** very.

182. **convented:** summoned.

184. **vulgarly;** publicly.

Most wrongfully accused your substitute,
Who is as free from touch or soil with her
As she from one ungot.   165
    Duke.   We did believe no less.
Know you that Friar Lodowick that she speaks of?
    Friar. I know him for a man divine and holy;
Not scurvy, nor a temporary meddler,
As he's reported by this gentleman;   170
And, on my trust, a man that never yet
Did, as he vouches, misreport your Grace.
    Lucio. My lord, most villainously; believe it.
    Friar. Well, he in time may come to clear himself;
But at this instant he is sick, my lord,   175
Of a strange fever. Upon his mere request—
Being come to knowledge that there was complaint
Intended 'gainst Lord Angelo—came I hither,
To speak, as from his mouth, what he doth know
Is true and false and what he with his oath   180
And all probation will make up full clear
Whensoever he's convented. First, for this woman,
To justify this worthy nobleman,
So vulgarly and personally accused,
Her shall you hear disproved to her eyes,   185
Till she herself confess it.
    Duke.   Good friar, let's hear it.
[*Isabella is carried off guarded; and Mariana comes
                                        forward.*]

Do you not smile at this, Lord Angelo?
O Heaven, the vanity of wretched fools!
Give us some seats. Come, cousin Angelo;   190

204. **punk:** prostitute.

208. **prattle for himself:** plead his own cause as foolishly.

212. **known:** i.e., carnally.

In this I'll be impartial: be you judge
Of your own cause. Is this the witness, friar?
First let her show her face and after speak.

 Mar. Pardon, my lord, I will not show my face
Until my husband bid me.   195

 Duke. What, are you married?

 Mar. No, my lord.

 Duke. Are you a maid?

 Mar. No, my lord.

 Duke. A widow, then?   200

 Mar. Neither, my lord.

 Duke. Why, you are nothing, then—neither maid,
widow, nor wife?

 Lucio. My lord, she may be a punk, for many of
them are neither maid, widow, nor wife.   205

 Duke. Silence that fellow. I would he had some
  cause
To prattle for himself.

 Lucio. Well, my lord.

 Mar. My lord, I do confess I ne'er was married;   210
And I confess, besides, I am no maid.
I have known my husband; yet my husband
Knows not that ever he knew me.

 Lucio. He was drunk, then, my lord: it can be no
better.   215

 Duke. For the benefit of silence, would thou wert
so too!

 Lucio. Well, my lord.

 Duke. This is no witness for Lord Angelo.

 Mar. Now I come to't, my lord: 220

226. **mo:** more; i.e., another man.
232. **abuse:** delusion or deception.

She that accuses him of fornication
In selfsame manner doth accuse my husband;
And charges him, my lord, with such a time
When I'll depose I had him in mine arms
With all the effect of love.   225
    Ang. Charges she mo than me?
    Mar.   Not that I know.
    Duke. No? You say your husband.
    Mar. Why, just, my lord, and that is Angelo,
Who thinks he knows that he ne'er knew my body, 230
But knows he thinks that he knows Isabel's.
    Ang. This is a strange abuse. Let's see thy face.
    Mar. My husband bids me; now I will unmask.
                                [*Unveiling.*]
This is that face, thou cruel Angelo,
Which once thou sworest was worth the looking on. 235
This is the hand which, with a vowed contract,
Was fast belocked in thine. This is the body
That took away the match from Isabel
And did supply thee at thy garden house
In her imagined person.   240
    Duke.   Know you this woman?
    Lucio. Carnally, she says.
    Duke.   Sirrah, no more!
    Lucio. Enough, my lord.
    Ang. My lord, I must confess I know this woman; 245
And five years since there was some speech of mar-
        riage
Betwixt myself and her, which was broke off,
Partly for that her promised proportions

252. **levity:** light (unchaste) behavior.
267. **scope:** full power.
269. **informal:** less than normal; deluded.
276. **Compact:** combined; allied.
279. **sealed in approbation:** certified by proof.

Came short of composition, but in chief   250
For that her reputation was disvalued
In levity. Since which time of five years
I never spake with her, saw her, nor heard from her,
Upon my faith and honor.

    Mar.   Noble prince,   255
As there comes light from Heaven and words from
    breath,
As there is sense in truth and truth in virtue,
I am affianced this man's wife as strongly
As words could make up vows. And, my good lord,   260
But Tuesday night last gone in's garden house
He knew me as a wife. As this is true,
Let me in safety raise me from my knees,
Or else forever be confixed here,
A marble monument!   265

    Ang.   I did but smile till now.
Now, good my lord, give me the scope of justice;
My patience here is touched. I do perceive
These poor informal women are no more
But instruments of some more mightier member   270
That sets them on. Let me have way, my lord,
To find this practice out.

    Duke.   Ay, with my heart;
And punish them to your height of pleasure.
Thou foolish friar, and thou pernicious woman,   275
Compact with her that's gone, thinkst thou thy oaths,
Though they would swear down each particular saint,
Were testimonies against his worth and credit
That's sealed in approbation? You, Lord Escalus,

295. **throughly:** thoroughly.

298. **Cucullus non facit monachum:** "a cowl does not make a monk," proverbial.

303. **notable:** worth noting (keeping an eye on).

Sit with my cousin: lend him your kind pains   280
To find out this abuse, whence 'tis derived.
There is another friar that set them on;
Let him be sent for.

   Friar. Would he were here, my lord! for he indeed
Hath set the women on to this complaint.   285
Your provost knows the place where he abides,
And he may fetch him.

   Duke.   Go, do it instantly.

                      [*Exit Provost.*]

And you, my noble and well-warranted cousin,
Whom it concerns to hear this matter forth,   290
Do with your injuries as seems you best,
In any chastisement. I for a while will leave you;
But stir not you till you have well determined
Upon these slanderers.

   Escal. My lord, we'll do it throughly. *Exit* [*Duke*]. 295
Signior Lucio, did not you say you knew that Friar
Lodowick to be a dishonest person?

   Lucio. *Cucullus non facit monachum:* honest in
nothing but in his clothes; and one that hath spoke
most villainous speeches of the Duke.   300

   Escal. We shall entreat you to abide here till he
come and enforce them against him. We shall find this
friar a notable fellow.

   Lucio. As any in Vienna, on my word.

   Escal. Call that same Isabel here once again: I 305
would speak with her. [*Exit an Attendant.*] Pray you,
my lord, give me leave to question. You shall see how
I'll handle her.

315. light: wanton.

Lucio. Not better than he, by her own report.

Escal. Say you?   310

Lucio. Marry, sir, I think, if you handled her privately, she would sooner confess: perchance, publicly, she'll be ashamed.

Ecal. I will go darkly to work with her.

Lucio. That's the way, for women are light at mid-   315
night.

*Enter Duke [in his friar's habit], Provost, Isabella
[with Officers].*

Escal. Come on, mistress: here's a gentlewoman denies all that you have said.

Lucio. My lord, here comes the rascal I spoke of;
here, with the provost.   320

Escal. In very good time: speak not you to him till we call upon you.

Lucio. Mum.

Escal. Come, sir: did you set these women on to slander Lord Angelo? They have confessed you did.   325

Duke. 'Tis false.

Escal. How! know you where you are?

Duke. Respect to your great place! and let the Devil
Be sometime honored for his burning throne!
Where is the Duke? 'Tis he should hear me speak.   330

Escal. The Duke's in us; and we will hear you
    speak.
Look you speak justly.

Duke. Boldly, at least. But, O, poor souls,

338. **retort**: reject.

348. **touse**: rack, tear.

354. **provincial**: subject to his authority.

357. **stew**: brothel.

359. **forfeits in a barber's shop**: i.e., teeth that have been extracted by the barber, which were then hung up in his shop—objects of ridicule rather than fear, having lost their power to bite.

A sixteenth-century dentist at work. Extracted teeth are strung to the dentist's sign at upper left. From Hartmann Schopper, *Panoplia* (1568).

Come you to seek the lamb here of the fox?   335
Good night to your redress! Is the Duke gone?
Then is your cause gone too. The Duke's unjust
Thus to retort your manifest appeal
And put your trial in the villain's mouth
Which here you come to accuse.   340
  Lucio. This is the rascal: this is he I spoke of.
  Escal. Why, thou unreverend and unhallowed friar,
Is't not enough thou hast suborned these women
To accuse this worthy man, but, in foul mouth,
And in the witness of his proper ear,   345
To call him villain? and then to glance from him
To the Duke himself, to tax him with injustice?
Take him hence; to the rack with him! We'll touse you
Joint by joint, but we will know his purpose.
What, "unjust"!   350
  Duke. Be not so hot: the Duke
Dare no more stretch this finger of mine than he
Dare rack his own. His subject am I not,
Nor here provincial. My business in this state
Made me a looker-on here in Vienna,   355
Where I have seen corruption boil and bubble
Till it o'errun the stew; laws for all faults,
But faults so countenanced that the strong statutes
Stand like the forfeits in a barber's shop,
As much in mock as mark.   360
  Escal. Slander to the state! Away with him to prison!
  Ang. What can you vouch against him, Signior
    Lucio?
Is this the man that you did tell us of?

372. **notedly:** precisely.
382. **close:** come to terms; back down.
387. **giglets:** light women.
388. **companion:** contemptible fellow.
394. **sheepbiting:** thievish.

Lucio. 'Tis he, my lord. Come hither, goodman 365
baldpate. Do you know me?

Duke. I remember you, sir, by the sound of your
voice. I met you at the prison, in the absence of the
Duke.

Lucio. O, did you so? And do you remember what 370
you said of the Duke?

Duke. Most notedly, sir.

Lucio. Do you so, sir? And was the Duke a flesh-
monger, a fool, and a coward, as you then reported
him to be? 375

Duke. You must, sir, change persons with me ere
you make that my report: you, indeed, spoke so of
him; and much more, much worse.

Lucio. O thou damnable fellow! Did not I pluck
thee by the nose for thy speeches? 380

Duke. I protest I love the Duke as I love myself.

Ang. Hark, how the villain would close now, after
his treasonable abuses!

Escal. Such a fellow is not to be talked withal.
Away with him to prison! Where is the provost? Away 385
with him to prison! Lay bolts enough upon him. Let
him speak no more. Away with those giglets too, and
with the other confederate companion!

Duke. [*To the provost*] Stay, sir; stay awhile.

Ang. What, resists he? Help him, Lucio. 390

Lucio. Come, sir; come, sir; come, sir! Foh, sir!
Why, you baldpated, lying rascal, you must
be hooded, must you? Show your knave's visage,
with a pox to you! Show your sheepbiting

407. **do thee office:** assist thee.
412. **undiscernible:** undetected.
414. **passes:** trespasses.

face, and be hanged an hour! Will't not off? 395
[*Pulls off the friar's hood, and discovers the Duke.*]
   Duke. Thou art the first knave that e'er madest a
     Duke.
First, provost, let me bail these gentle three.
[*To Lucio*] Sneak not away, sir, for the friar and you
Must have a word anon. Lay hold on him. 400
   Lucio. This may prove worse than hanging.
   Duke. [*To Escalus*] What you have spoke I pardon.
     Sit you down:
We'll borrow place of him. [*To Angelo*] Sir, by your
     leave. 405
Hast thou or word, or wit, or impudence,
That yet can do thee office? If thou hast,
Rely upon it till my tale be heard,
And hold no longer out.
   Ang.   O my dread lord, 410
I should be guiltier than my guiltiness,
To think I can be undiscernible,
When I perceive your Grace, like pow'r divine,
Hath looked upon my passes. Then, good prince,
No longer session hold upon my shame, 415
But let my trial be mine own confession:
Immediate sentence, then, and sequent death,
Is all the grace I beg.
   Duke.   Come hither, Mariana.
Say, wast thou e'er contracted to this woman? 420
   Ang. I was, my lord.
   Duke. Go take her hence and marry her instantly.

423. **consummate:** performed.
429. **Advertising and holy:** acting as a dedicated adviser.
431. **Attorneyed:** enlisted as an attorney.
436. **free:** generous.
440. **rash remonstrance:** speedy revelation.
444. **brained:** killed.

Do you the office, friar; which consummate,
Return him here again. Go with him, provost.
    Exeunt [Angelo, Mariana, Friar Peter and Provost].
    Escal. My lord, I am more amazed at his dishonor   425
Than at the strangeness of it.
    Duke.   Come hither, Isabel.
Your friar is now your prince. As I was then
Advertising and holy to your business,
Not changing heart with habit, I am still   430
Attorneyed at your service.
    Isa.   O, give me pardon,
That I, your vassal, have employed and pained
Your unknown sovereignty!
    Duke.   You are pardoned, Isabel.   435
And now, dear maid, be you as free to us.
Your brother's death, I know, sits at your heart;
And you may marvel why I obscured myself,
Laboring to save his life, and would not rather
Make rash remonstrance of my hidden power   440
Than let him so be lost. O most kind maid,
It was the swift celerity of his death,
Which I did think with slower foot came on,
That brained my purpose. But, peace be with him!
That life is better life, past fearing death,   445
Than that which lives to fear. Make it your comfort,
So happy is your brother.
    Isa.   I do, my lord.

Enter Angelo, Mariana, [Friar] Peter, [and] Provost.

450. **salt:** lustful.

457. **proper:** own.

460. **Measure still for Measure:** this phrase and the play's title derive from Matt. 7:20.

462–63. **denies thee vantage:** i.e., the fault being manifest, denial cannot help him.

468. **mock me with a husband:** i.e., give me a husband only to snatch him away.

Duke. For this new-married man, approaching here,
Whose salt imagination yet hath wronged   450
Your well-defended honor, you must pardon
For Mariana's sake: but as he adjudged your brother—
Being criminal, in double violation
Of sacred chastity and of promise-breach
Thereon dependent—for your brother's life   455
The very mercy of the law cries out
Most audible, even from his proper tongue,
"An Angelo for Claudio, death for death!"
Haste still pays haste, and leisure answers leisure;
Like doth quit like, and Measure still for Measure.   460
Then, Angelo, thy fault's thus manifested;
Which, though thou wouldst deny, denies thee
        vantage.
We do condemn thee to the very block
Where Claudio stooped to death, and with like haste.   465
Away with him!

  Mar.   O my most gracious lord,
I hope you will not mock me with a husband.

  Duke. It is your husband mocked you with a hus-
        band.   470
Consenting to the safeguard of your honor,
I thought your marriage fit; else imputation
For that he knew you might reproach your life
And choke your good to come. For his possessions,
Although by confiscation they are ours,   475
We do instate and widow you withal,
To buy you a better husband.

480. **definitive:** determined.
488. **fact:** deed.
489. **paved:** covered with a stone slab.
495. **for the most:** usually.

 Mar.   O my dear lord,
I crave no other, nor no better man.
 Duke. Never crave him. We are definitive.   480
 Mar. [*Kneeling*] Gentle my liege—
 Duke.   You do but lose your labor.
Away with him to death! [*To Lucio*] Now, sir, to you.
 Mar. O my good lord! Sweet Isabel, take my part:
Lend me your knees, and all my life to come   485
I'll lend you all my life to do you service.
 Duke. Against all sense you do importune her.
Should she kneel down in mercy of this fact,
Her brother's ghost his paved bed would break
And take her hence in horror.   490
 Mar.   Isabel,
Sweet Isabel, do yet but kneel by me;
Hold up your hands, say nothing, I'll speak all.
They say, best men are molded out of faults,
And, for the most, become much more the better 495
For being a little bad. So may my husband.
O Isabel, will you not lend a knee?
 Duke. He dies for Claudio's death.
 Isa. [*Kneeling*]   Most bounteous sir,
Look, if it please you, on this man condemned 500
As if my brother lived. I partly think
A due sincerity governed his deeds,
Till he did look on me. Since it is so,
Let him not die. My brother had but justice,
In that he did the thing for which he died.   505
For Angelo,
His act did not o'ertake his bad intent,

509. **Thoughts are no subjects:** i.e., "thought is free," a proverbial idea.

523. **more advice:** further consideration.

532. **still:** always.

And must be buried but as an intent
That perished by the way. Thoughts are no subjects,
Intents but merely thoughts.   510
    Mar.   Merely, my lord.
    Duke. Your suit's unprofitable. Stand up, I say.
I have bethought me of another fault.
Provost, how came it Claudio was beheaded
At an unusual hour?   515
    Pro.   It was commanded so.
    Duke. Had you a special warrant for the deed?
    Pro. No, my good lord: it was by private message.
    Duke. For which I do discharge you of your office.
Give up your keys.   520
    Pro.   Pardon me, noble lord.
I thought it was a fault, but knew it not;
Yet did repent me, after more advice.
For testimony whereof, one in the prison,
That should by private order else have died,   525
I have reserved alive.
    Duke.   What's he?
    Pro.   His name is Barnardine.
    Duke. I would thou hadst done so by Claudio.
Go fetch him hither. Let me look upon him.   530
                            [Exit Provost.]
    Escal. I am sorry one so learned and so wise
As you, Lord Angelo, have still appeared,
Should slip so grossly, both in the heat of blood
And lack of tempered judgment afterward.
    Ang. I am sorry that such sorrow I procure;   535
And so deep sticks it in my penitent heart

544. **squarest:** shapest.
545. **quit:** forgive.
559. **quits:** requites; repays.
561. **apt remission:** ready forgiveness.

That I crave death more willingly than mercy:
'Tis my deserving, and I do entreat it.

Enter Barnardine and Provost, Claudio [muffled, and]
Juliet.

  Duke. Which is that Barnardine?
  Pro.   This, my lord.   540
  Duke. There was a friar told me of this man.
Sirrah, thou art said to have a stubborn soul
That apprehends no further than this world
And squarest thy life according. Thou'rt condemned:
But, for those earthly faults, I quit them all;   545
And pray thee take this mercy to provide
For better times to come. Friar, advise him;
I leave him to your hand. What muffled fellow's that?
  Pro. This is another prisoner that I saved,
Who should have died when Claudio lost his head; 550
As like almost to Claudio as himself.
                         [Unmuffles Claudio.]
  Duke. [*To Isabella*] If he be like your brother, for
  his sake
Is he pardoned; and, for your lovely sake—
Give me your hand and say you will be mine—   555
He is my brother too: but fitter time for that.
By this Lord Angelo perceives he's safe:
Methinks I see a quick'ning in his eye.
Well, Angelo, your evil quits you well.
Look that you love your wife; her worth, worth yours. 560
I find an apt remission in myself;

565. **luxury:** lust.

568–69. **according to the trick:** after my habitual fashion.

581. **cuckold:** husband with an unchaste wife.

586–87. **pressing to death:** the contemporary penalty for refusing to plead.

The pressing to death of Griffin Flood for refusing to plead. From *The Life and Death of Griffin Flood* (1623).

And yet here's one in place I cannot pardon.
[*To Lucio*] You, sirrah, that knew me for a fool, a
    coward,
One all of luxury, an ass, a madman;   565
Wherein have I so deserved of you,
That you extol me thus?
    Lucio. Faith, my lord, I spoke it but according to
the trick. If you will hang me for it, you may; but I
had rather it would please you I might be whipt. 570
    Duke. Whipt first, sir, and hanged after.
Proclaim it, provost, round about the city,
If any woman wronged by this lewd fellow—
As I have heard him swear himself there's one
Whom he begot with child—let her appear,   575
And he shall marry her: the nuptial finished,
Let him be whipt and hanged.
    Lucio. I beseech your Highness, do not marry me
to a whore. Your Highness said even now I made you
a Duke: good my lord, do not recompense me in 580
making me a cuckold.
    Duke. Upon mine honor, thou shalt marry her.
Thy slanders I forgive; and therewithal
Remit thy other forfeits. Take him to prison;
And see our pleasure herein executed.   585
    Lucio. Marrying a punk, my lord, is pressing to
death, whipping, and hanging.
    Duke. Slandering a prince deserves it.
                [*Exeunt Officers with Lucio.*]
She, Claudio, that you wronged, look you restore.
Joy to you, Mariana! Love her, Angelo.   590

593. **behind:** to come; **gratulate:** gratifying.
599. **motion much imports your good:** suggestion tending to your great benefit.

I have confessed her, and I know her virtue.
Thanks, good friend Escalus, for thy much goodness.
There's more behind that is more gratulate.
Thanks, provost, for thy care and secrecy:
We shall employ thee in a worthier place.   595
Forgive him, Angelo, that brought you home
The head of Ragozine for Claudio's:
The offense pardons itself. Dear Isabel,
I have a motion much imports your good;
Whereto if you'll a willing ear incline,   600
What's mine is yours, and what is yours is mine.
So, bring us to our palace, where we'll show
What's yet behind that's meet you all should know.
                             [*Exeunt.*]

MEAT

CARNALITY

KEY TO
Famous Passages

Spirits are not finely touched
But to fine issues.   [*Duke*—I. i. 37–38]

Thus can the demigod Authority
Make us pay down for our offense by weight
The words of Heaven: on whom it will, it will;
On whom it will not, so. Yet still 'tis just.
                        [*Claudio*—I. ii. 121–24]

As surfeit is the father of much fast,
So every scope by the immoderate use
Turns to restraint. Our natures do pursue,
Like rats that ravin down their proper bane,
A thirsty evil; and when we drink, we die.
                        [*Claudio*—I. ii. 128–32]

Liberty plucks Justice by the nose,
The baby beats the nurse, and quite athwart
Goes all decorum.   [*Duke*—I. iii. 30–32]

Lord Angelo is precise;
Stands at a guard with envy; scarce confesses
That his blood flows or that his appetite
Is more to bread than stone.   [*Duke*—I. iii. 53–56]

I'll be supposed upon a book, his face is
the worst thing about him.   [*Pompey*—II. i. 158–59]

No ceremony that to great ones 'longs,
Not the king's crown nor the deputed sword,
The marshal's truncheon nor the judge's robe,
Become them with one half so good a grace
As mercy does.   [*Isabella*—II. ii. 77–81]

Why, all the souls that were, were forfeit once;
And He that might the vantage best have took
Found out the remedy. How would you be
If He, which is the top of judgment, should
But judge you as you are? O, think on that,
And mercy then will breathe within your lips
Like man new made.   *[Isabella*—II. ii. 95–101]

Man, proud man,
Drest in a little brief authority,
Most ignorant of what he's most assured,
His glassy essence, like an angry ape
Plays such fantastic tricks before high Heaven
As makes the angels weep.   *[Isabella*—II. ii. 145–50]

O cunning enemy that to catch a saint
With saints dost bait thy hook!   *[Angelo*—II. ii. 220–21]

Thou hast nor youth nor age,
But, as it were, an after-dinner's sleep,
Dreaming on both.   *[Duke*—III. i. 33–36]

If I must die,
I will encounter darkness as a bride
And hug it in mine arms.   *[Claudio*—III. i. 95–97]

Ay, but to die and go we know not where;
To lie in cold obstruction and to rot,
This sensible warm motion to become
A kneaded clod; and the delighted spirit
To bathe in fiery floods, or to reside
In thrilling region of thick-ribbed ice;
To be imprisoned in the viewless winds
And blown with restless violence round about
The pendent world. . . .
The weariest and most loathed worldly life
That age, ache, penury, and imprisonment
Can lay on nature is a paradise
To what we fear of death.   *[Claudio*—III. i. 137–51]

Take, O, take those lips away,
  That so sweetly were forsworn.   [*Song*—IV. i. 1–6]

Haste still pays haste, and leisure answers
  leisure;
Like doth quit like, and Measure still for
  Measure.   [*Duke*—V. i. 459–60]

Shakespeare's
Immortal Comedies And Romances

THE FOLGER LIBRARY GENERAL READER'S SHAKESPEARE

The Folger single volume editions are the standard editions for students and general readers alike. Conveniently printed on right-hand pages with notes on facing pages; includes plot summaries, explanatory notes, essays and historical information.

Build your Shakespeare library with these handsomely-illustrated and fully-annotated volumes.

THE COMEDIES
ALL'S WELL THAT ENDS WELL 41891/$2.25
AS YOU LIKE IT 45913/$2.50
COMEDY OF ERRORS 46717/$2.95
MEASURE FOR MEASURE 49612/$2.95
THE MERCHANT OF VENICE 49178/$2.95
MERRY WIVES OF WINDSOR 42139/$2.25
MIDSUMMER NIGHT'S DREAM 43297/$2.25
MUCH ADO ABOUT NOTHING 44722/$2.25
TAMING OF THE SHREW 47717/$2.95
TWELFTH NIGHT 45752/$2.50
TROILUS AND CRESSIDA 49116/$1.95

THE ROMANCES
CYMBELINE 49112/$1.95
PERICLES 49118/$1.95
THE TEMPEST 49618/$2.50
THE WINTER'S TALE 42195/$2.50

WASHINGTON SQUARE PRESS